Alfred Austin

The tower of Babel

A celestial love-drama

Alfred Austin

The tower of Babel
A celestial love-drama

ISBN/EAN: 9783337335366

Printed in Europe, USA, Canada, Australia, Japan

Cover: Foto ©Andreas Hilbeck / pixelio.de

More available books at **www.hansebooks.com**

THE

TOWER OF BABEL

A Celestial Love=Drama

BY

ALFRED AUSTIN

And it came to pass, as they journeyed from the East, that they found a plain in the land of Shinar; and they dwelt there. And they said one to another, Go to, let us make brick, and burn them throughly. And they had brick for stone, and slime had they for mortar. And they said, Go to, let us build us a city, and a tower whose top may reach unto heaven. —GENESIS xi. 2-4.

London

MACMILLAN AND CO.

AND NEW YORK

1890

DEDICATION

THE EARL OF LYTTON, G.C.B.

MY DEAR LYTTON,

It is not in my power to add to the distinctions that have attended you in the course of your career. Born to eminence by the genius of your sire, you have not slumbered ingloriously under the shelter of his fame. More various in your achievements even than those *quibus deorum munere datum est aut facere scribenda, aut scribere legenda,* you have not only enriched the literature, you have likewise extended the authority, of your country.

I have a much less presumptuous motive in asking you to accept the dedication of this work.

It is offered less to the author of *The Wanderer*
and *Glenaveril*, or to the Viceroy who applied,
and in part conceived, an Indian Frontier Policy
vehemently arraigned at the time, but now acknow-
ledged to have been wise and far-seeing, than to the
genial friend and the generous critic. Whether your
contemporaries have done you ample justice, posterity
will decide with infallible discrimination. But this I
do know, that of all your contemporaries alike you
are the most magnanimous judge I have ever met.

I have no right to expect that others who may
happen to read this volume will bring to the perusal
of it that indulgent sympathy which, in your case, has
been unblunted by creative energy. Composed seven-
teen years ago with that impulsive exuberance for
which the measured judgment of maturer life is an
imperfect compensation, and now severely revised, it
seems to me to represent, in theme at least, one of
the permanent aspects of human society. Man will
never cease to build Towers of Babel; and his
Heaven-defying architecture has in this age been even
unusually ambitious. Happily, the mystery which
stimulated our progenitors in the land of Shinar still
remains unsolved; for, as you have yourself said—

" .   .   . The Unknown
Is life to Love, Religion, Poetry."

Happily, too, though neither materialists nor meta-
physicians may get us any nearer to the sky, Seraphim
perpetually descend from it ; and humble souls, who,
after all, are the only wise ones, will, I trust, see in
Aran's failure nothing to lament, or find at least in
the union of Afrael and Noema ample consolation.

Believe me, My dear Lytton,

With every cordial good wish,

. Yours most faithfully,

ALFRED AUSTIN.

Swinford Old Manor,
October 1890.

PERSONAGES

ARAN, the Chief Builder of the Tower.

NOEMA, his wife.

IRAD, their son : a boy of seven.

SIDON, a Philosopher.

EBER, an Astrologer.

KORAH, an Enthusiast and Believer in Perfectibility.

PELEG, a Priest.

FREEMEN—BONDMEN.

AFRAEL, a Spirit.

VOICES OF THE AIR.

Scene of the Drama—The Plain of Shinar.

Time—The twenty-third century before Christ.

ACT I

SCENE I

Evening.   The tents of ARAN.   NOEMA and IRAD in front of the chief tent.

NOEMA.

COME, Irad, come, the hour for rest is here ;
The sun is no more with us, and the west,
Through   the   moist   air,   glows   like   your   cheeks
     bedewed
With the sweet sweat of pastime's unpaid toil,
And the first star peers o'er the mountain-peak.
The very birds are sleeping ; why not you ?
You must to rest.

IRAD.

I am not tired, mother.

B

One little moment more, just one, I beg,
Then will I come.   I should not sleep; indeed
I never was more wakeful.   And then see,
I have not finished building up my tower,
Which lacks its roof.   One second more, just one.

NOEMA.

Well, just a second, Irad. . . . Strange ! how strange !
Childhood should chafe 'gainst manhood's kindest
        friend,
And sleep, which wooeth carelessness, should be
By carelessness repelled ! while care, rich care,
Would give its flocks and herds, ay, all its store,
So might it drop its leaden plummet down,
For one brief night, into the depths of slumber.
Oh, may the eve ne'er come to you, my child,
When you shall call on sleep, and find it deaf
Even as the ear of one you are pining for,
And cannot move : deaf as that stony Fate
At whose closed door our hearts still thump in vain !
Now, Irad, come, and till to-morrow leave
Your toys and sports, and pray at mother's knee,
And she will smooth the pillow of your crib,
And sing your eyelids into drowsiness.

IRAD.

But father said that I might wait for him :
He will be coming soon.

NOEMA.

He will be late,—
Too late, to-night, for you to bide his coming ;
But he shall visit your repose, and breathe
A father's blessing on your innocent dreams.
Hearken, dear Irad, to your mother's voice,
And do her bidding.

IRAD.

Always, mother dear !
I only thought you had not overheard
What father said,—that I might wait for him.
Why should he be so late to-night ?   You know
It is the season he is home betimes ;
What keeps him, mother ?

NOEMA (*aside*).

Oh, he must not know :
He must not know   How shall I answer him ?
What keeps your father, did you ask ?   Why, child,

A round of things, as you will know some day,
When life no longer splits in equal halves
Of sleep and pastime. . . . Now, unto your prayer.

IRAD.

Yes, mother, straight.   But let me show you first
My tower,—the tower which I myself have made
With my own hands.   Look there !

>   [IRAD holds up a miniature tower in fresh clay.

NOEMA.

Why, what is this ?
Why have you made so trivial a toy,
When you have scores of playthings, fairer far ?

IRAD.

It is for use, not beauty, mother.   This,
This is the tower that is to scale the skies,
And bring us riches without stint or toil.

NOEMA.

He has told him, then ! told him, despite my prayer,
And from this budding blossom torn away
The tender hull, making an entrance there
For cankering thought and blight rebellious !

With unpaternal hands man's poison poured
Into the limpid life of infancy,
And dropped infection in the very veins
He should have saved from such contagion !
Oh ! impious !

> [She lets the tower fall, which breaks into fragments.

IRAD.

O mother ! see ! you have destroyed my tower.

NOEMA.

Yes ! as the high God will that Tower destroy
With which they think to pierce the firmament,
And wrench the enclosed lightnings from His grasp.
Oh, it is madness !   Men *are* mad sometimes,
And from the heights of strength they topple over
Into insanity.   No more of it !
Your father did not mean to tell you, Irad,
And he has changed his purpose since the morning :
Be sure of that. . . . And, Irad, never again
Defile your little hands with such gross work,
That were but given you to be clasped in prayer.
Now kneel, and fold them, and repeat with awe
The words I taught you ere your lips had ceased

To do their double duty at my breast,
Of feeding you with life and me with joy.
Begin.

IRAD (*kneeling at her feet and praying aloud*).

Almighty Being, That dost dwell
In the high Heavens apart,
Alone, and inaccessible
Save to the seeing heart ;
Shelter our herds, increase our flocks,
Ripen the swelling grain,
Breathe life into the barren rocks,
And send the timely rain.

Grant to my father length of days,
And to my mother give
A spirit meek, that in Thy gaze
She humbly still may live !
Cause me to feel, through good, through ill,
How poor a thing am I,
And, when I have fulfilled Thy will,
Resignedly to die.

NOEMA (*kissing* IRAD *tenderly*).

Dear one ! 'twas sweetly said.   O Irad ! never

Be these petitions from your lips divorced,

So you would love me.

IRAD.

Never shall they, mother !

NOEMA.

Then let me fold you snugly in your nest ;

And the still Night shall be your canopy,

Like a broad branch which hangs, but never moves,

Over some absent song-bird's unfledged brood.

> [Mother and Child go into the tent.   The last streaks
> of sunset disappear, and an intense twilight follows,
> which infuses into the air and sky a deeper radiance.
> NOEMA returns alone, and gazes out with an air of
> melancholy.

SCENE II

NOEMA.

How beautiful !   The lately solid earth

Hath lost its look of gross reality,

And, like the air, waxeth impalpable.

The foliaged trees seem shapes of atmosphere,

And the tall trunks themselves mere bars of light.

The hill-tops and the firmament have blent

In crimson hush of close communion.

There is no sound, save the Euphrates flowing,

Which casts the silence into deeper shade ;

And, overhead, the sky is so transparent,

It seems a wonder that I see not through ;

Save that I chance were blinded if I saw

What lies the other side. . . . How beautiful!

It is the hour when, in my inmost being,

I feel a something alien to myself,

Which sets me against self rebellious :

A consciousness of kindred unallowed

With the moist gloaming, with the far-off sky,

And advent of the silent-speaking stars :

A leaven of unrest, a dumb desire,

A wistfulness of longing that I might

Slough off this torpid chrysalis of flesh,

And nothing be but wings and gossamer

Blown through the empty spaces of the air!

O words! poor words! how behind thought you
      lag!

Like crippled forms that, still importunate,

With hurrying gait and plaintive breath pursue,

But cannot catch us up ! . . . In such a strait,
Silence and sighs alone are eloquent.

> [She sits rapt in contemplation.   At length she speaks
> again.

How strangely bright gloweth the star of eve !
Surely it never burned so bright since first
God's summons called it from the starless void.
How near it seems ! and every moment nearer !
Yet no ! 'tis not the star that moves, but rather,
An arrowy scintillation darting down
The unresisting air.   Withal, 'tis not
A shooting star ; for, see ! it is not quenched
In its own flight, but still, as it descends,
Grows larger, larger, yet less luminous.
It is no star.   It wears half mortal mien.
It is a wingèd Spirit that doth come,
Commissioned with celestial messages,
Or some belated denizen of air
Strayed far beyond the heavenly boundaries.
How motionless it poises, as in doubt
If to touch earth or sail away again.
Lo ! it descends, and on the shell alights
Of this gross sphere.   How like, yet how unlike,
One in whose garb youth and first manhood meet,

When beauty shares with strength dominion,

And knowledge gains the ear of innocence.

Yet ne'er was mortal brow like that, which wears

No touch of sadness and no trace of toil;

And, though his limbs have form, I can no more

Betwixt them and the air discriminate,

Than, in this hour, betwixt the day and night.

He doth not yet perceive me, though his feet,

Silent, and slow, and musically move

More closely toward me. . . . Yes, it is a Spirit;

For he is naked, yet he knows no shame,

And I no fear.   I wonder will he speak to me?

It may be I am too corporeal

For spiritual sight.

       [The Spirit perceives NOEMA and advances towards her.

AFRAEL.

What star is this?

NOEMA.

This is no star, this is the Earth thou seest.

AFRAEL.

Then in the thought of Spirits how 'tis wronged!

They fancy Earth misshapen, foul, and rude,
Of disposition most ungenial;
Worse and most worthless of the worlds, and left
To be the sport of spiteful elements.
But it is fair as any single orb
That I have scanned in my discursive flights
Among the planetary spheres that roll
Glibly upon the unsubstantial air.

NOEMA.

Yes, it is fair sometimes, and hath this eve
Assumed a bright complexion, as though it did
Await some swift superior visitant.
I would my lord were nigh to bid you cheer.
To such a lofty guest even man would plead
His imperfection; but a woman's state
Too lowly is to welcome you, or crave
Excuse for such a greeting.

AFRAEL.

               You are meek,
Nor could I wish for any to amend
Your salutation. But wherein do men,
Of whom you speak, differ from such as you?

NOEMA.

Men are our sterner, stronger selves, to whom
We reverence pay and mute obedience ;
And our volitions with their will they curb,
As Heaven curbs Earth.

AFRAEL.

Men must be godlike, then ?

NOEMA.

'Tis said they are.   I have not found them so.
But they are stout of limb and stern of heart,
Intrepid, stalwart, nigh invincible,
Bearding obstruction, while we crouch at home,
And drop our feeble tears upon the ground.
For us they work, and we to them belong,
As scents and blossoms to the strenuous breeze,
Which wafts them where it will, nor reason gives
Save power to do it.

AFRAEL.

I would I were a man !

NOEMA.

What !   You !—a Spirit !—be a man, and pay

The forfeit of your immortality !
We do not live for ever, as Spirits live.

AFRAEL.

Not live for ever !   What, then, do ye do ?

NOEMA.

We die, women and men.

AFRAEL.

What is to die ?

NOEMA.

It is to bid adieu to joy and pain,
And never nurse them more : to sleep with Night,
Nor to awake from its cold-clutching arms ;
Never to see the sun again, nor greet
The rising moon with rapture, nor the stars
With eyes self-blinded in delicious tears.

AFRAEL.

But you, *you* will not die !

NOEMA.

O yes, I shall.
The worms will have my cheeks, the dust my lips,

And in the socket of mine eyes the snail
Snugly itself ensconce.   As for my voice,
'Twill, like the nightingale's, break off, but never,
Like to the nightingale's, its note resume,
But perish on the unsympathising air.

AFRAEL.

Then all your sort will in the end die out,
And this fair Earth be left untenanted.

NOEMA.

Not so.   Our race doth still renew itself
By means unknown to Spirits.   Man's delight
Is to embrace these carnal substances,
Your thought too much extols ; and woman's is
The passionate joy of pain that ends in joy
From which all pain hath passed : to bear him sons,
Who shall repeat the vigour of their sire,
And daughters who shall wax to comeliness,
And warm with pride his chill declining years,
Then when their mother comely is no more.
And this is compensation e'en for death,—
To feel the little lips tight on one's breast,
To have the little arms around one's throat,

And hear the little voice lisping one's name
In efforts made by love articulate.
This is pure bliss !

AFRAEL.

And you have known it ?

NOEMA.

Yes.

AFRAEL.

Have you sons and daughters then ?

NOEMA.

I have a son,

Just one : a little fellow, fast asleep,
Whom I had kissed and lullabied to rest,
Just ere you came.

AFRAEL.

He must be fair as Heaven,

If he resembles you.

    [NOEMA goes into the tent and brings out IRAD, in her
       arms, asleep.

AFRAEL (*with a look of disappointment*).

A pretty thing.
But he hath swarthy cheeks and ebon curls,
And is not of your seeming.

NOEMA.   ·

'Tis because
His father mostly lives in him.

AFRAEL.

But why
Are his lids closed, and he so motionless?
This is not death?

NOEMA.

My darling dead!   Forefend
That such a stroke befall! that I should lose
Who is to me what dew is to the flowers,
Themselves distil, and are fed back by it.
This is the daily mimicry of death,
Without its closing action.   This is sleep.
I wish that you could see him at his play.

[She carries IRAD back into the tent and returns without
him.

AFRAEL.

I would ask more.   Spirits are curious :
To feel and know is all our appetite.
And I would learn if men and women have
The power to fashion creatures like themselves,
And multiply their image, as they will.

NOEMA.

They have that power.

AFRAEL.

Why then indeed ye are
Liker to God than any I have heard of.

NOEMA.

We have the dark dread power to conjure life,
But not to keep alive ; and mortal fates
Are no more godlike than the leaves that fall,
When fresh leaves come from the same origin.

AFRAEL.

There's something stranger here than you conceive.
For if the dimpled cherub whom I saw
With folded wings but now within your arms,

C

Be born of you, why are you not like leaves
Whom new leaves threaten,—sapless, shrunk, and
    sere ?
You have a something Spirits do not have,
Who know nor fruit nor blight and ever keep
The blossom of existence, first they wear ;
For, though unlike to these, and as to me
It seems, superior far, you still are young,
And own the dewy radiance of the morn.

NOEMA.

I am nor young nor old, mortals would say :
A mother mid-way betwixt youth and age,
Like to the moon, when yet but half eclipsed.

AFRAEL.

It needs must be they see with mortal eyes,
For, to my seeing, youth and age have met,
By some divine attraction, in your cheeks,
And made a rare complexion.   All excess,
As all defect, is banished from your brow,
And you are perfect in your motherhood.
Oh, I could stay and praise you through the night,
If skies were not importunate, nor I

Must needs,—as loth I never felt before,—
Take all unwillingly my heavenward way.

NOEMA.

Have you a lodge in Heaven, and yet can want
To be a tenant for one instant here,
Where there breathes nought but want unsatisfied,
And bliss that bursts like bubbles in the blowing?
Can that strange malady of mortal blood,
Which still unweds us from ourselves, and woos
That which with self will ne'er amalgamate,
Infect the veins of Spirits?   Your abode
Is in the Heaven of Heavens.   What's Earth to
    you?

AFRAEL.

The only Heaven that I yet have seen !
You misconceive.   I am not of the blest,
If such there be,—and if there be, no more
Envy I them,—who see the face of God.
The stars which are fast tingling into sight,
And myriads which you do not scan, are all
The native spot of Spirits, and I dwell
In one of these, whither I now return.

But if there be sweet kindliness on Earth,
It must within your bosom have found space;
And, are you kindly, you will bid my feet
Again be lost where you will still be found.
Say, will my wings be welcome?

NOEMA.

　　　　　　　　Nought so much.

But see! on yon horizon I behold
My lord approaching.　Will you wait for him?

AFRAEL.

No, not this eve.

NOEMA.

　　　　Forgive me if I err,

Through human appetite; and Spirits perchance
Live not as we.　But I have fruit, and wine,
Bread, and fresh herbs, if you will eat of them.

AFRAEL.

What doth sustain such loveliness as yours,
Could for no Spirit be unmeet.　Withal
We live upon the Universe we see,
And drink its all-sufficing elements.

The glory of the heavens when they open,
Slowly before the up-coming of the sun,
The warmth of mid-day skies, the moist decline
Of drooping day, the nightly silences,
And music of the many-cadenced rain,
Colour, and light, and shapes fantastical
Of plain, and hill, and cloudy pinnacle,
And ever-shifting subtleties of air,
All that we see and feel of fair and far,
Is to us sustenance, as I this eve
Have on your beauty made a rare repast ;
Which other Spirits will nourish, when to-night
We sit amid the watch-fires of the skies,
And tell each other tales of all the worlds.
And I shall tell of your strange loveliness,
Fair, melancholy mortal !

> [He raises and waves his wings over NOEMA, and soars
> into the air singing.

NOEMA.

How dulcetly he sings, still as he soars,
As though his wings were buoyed by melody,
And music were the wind that wafts him on !
Likely he singeth yet, though now, alas !

The heavenly distance to my clouded sense
Denies the strain, and I can but descry,
Dimly, the outline of celestial limbs,
Cleaving the twilight on the sails of song.
Alack ! he dwindles, glimmering, into space,
And lo ! evanishes ; and though I cling
With straining eyes into that point of air
Where last he glowed, then glimmered, I behold
Only the skyey vista tenantless.
O that I knew in what bright star he dwells,
That I might gaze towards him with fixed eyes;
And watch at least the road whereby he went !
I never thought to ask him ; for my lips,
As he discoursed, deferring to my ears,
Which drank his honeyed questioning, forgot .
To ply their curious office.   So I gaze
Into the darkness, and surmise him not,
Nor whitherward he turned his final way.
Yet he hath left a something in the air,
A something all around me that was not
Here ere his coming, and which lingers still.
Behind his blank departure : something soft,
And warm, and near, as unseen odours are.
I felt it when he o'er me waved his wings,

Just ere his lightsome feet forsook the Earth,

And, rising, took their native element :

I feel it still !

> [ARAN approaches.   NOEMA rises, and advances duti-
> fully towards him.

SCENE III

NOEMA.

Welcome, my spouse and lord !

ARAN.

Is the meal drest ?

NOEMA.

It is, and waits within.

ARAN.

Then let us to it at once.   I crave for food,

And drink, and rest, and truce to weariness.

NOEMA.

My lord is spent with toil.

ARAN.

Who would not be?
But there be toils shall have an end, and mar
The stern Taskmaster's trade for whom we slave,
Son after sire, age after age, unpaid
Save with the pittance of life's menial wage.
No longer will we bear the daily dole
Of food and sleep, ending in famished death.
If there be God or Gods, Gods will we be,
Not slowly-dying drudges.   Soon the Tower
Will mount in surging spirals to the sky,
And from its tall intrepid battlements
Will we storm Heaven, its tyranny dislodge,
Or with it strike a compact that shall yield
Its secrets to our knowledge, and secure
Wealth without sweat, and life unplagued by death.
Ay, we have done a good day's work this day,
Though none have paid us for our husbandry.

NOEMA.

Your words wing shafts of terror to my heart.
Assailing Heaven, you do but build for Hell,
And the foundations of your Tower will sink

Where Lucifer and all his rebels lie,
Farther from hope than worst mortality.

ARAN.

Then let us sink, if sink in sooth we must,
But not till after exercise of strength
That shall torment His anger, and at least
Ruffle the surface of His proud neglect :
Not die, like camels, underneath the load
We to the journey's end submissive bore,
Because our hearts were steeped in sufferance.
'Tis something to be whelmed in endless Hell,
And nourish hate, not Hell itself can quench ;
No, nor yet Heaven !   But still to be a thing
To moil and die 'neath Heaven's indifference—
This is a doom weak women well may bear.
We were no longer men, did we endure it !

NOEMA.

And yet it is a doom which, Aran, you,
And yours, and all mankind must bear.   Do you think
That to suit mortal passion Heaven will make
Mortals immortal, even for woe and wrath ?
Spirits have immortality of joy,

And demons immortality of pain.
But we, a lesser and a lower race,
An adumbration of the two and set
Betwixt the upper and the nether world,
In this frail compound even mixtures own
Of joy that passes and of pain that dies.
This is man's lot : nothing will alter it.

ARAN.

Nothing can leave it worse.   So will we strive
To make it better.   For we can but die,
Or still live baffled, as we are baffled now.
And what is it we ask ?   Pale dreamers may
Demand the eternal secrets : I, for one,
Claim food, and drink, and raiment, and the joys
Which come of fulness, ease, and certainty ;
A life of even pleasure, edged with death,
When these can please no more.   'Tis all I seek.

NOEMA.

That were a sordid craving.   Is it for these
That you arraign the Lord Omnipotent,—
That, having made you man, He did not make
You wholly beastlike ?   O, sir ! pardon me

If I fall short of duty !   But your aims,
Thus carnally contained, revolt me more
Than if you blasphemously should aspire
To be nor beast nor man, but very God !

ARAN.

Ay, ay, I pardon you : I pity rather.
These are the morbid fantasies which find
An empty chamber in your woman's brain,
And therein scamper idly. . . . Carnal aims !
Be very God !   Who builds a Tower, *now* ?
You have the same disease as we in sooth,
But, us unlike, know not its name nor cure.
Fine words are women's drapery for facts.
We call it misery ; you call it woe.
We curse our wrongs and pain, while you drop tears,
Bootless as dew, over the canker, grief.

NOEMA.

Nay, call not grief a canker !   Canker kills,
But grief still makes us cruelly alive,
And our most torpid pulses sensitive ;
Doubles the day by banishing the night,
And chokes us with each mouthful ; while Time sits,

Droning his weary minutes in our ears,

Till every second seemeth infinite,

Ay, longer than whole centuries of joy.

If grief would murder, 'twere no longer grief;

But it prefers to torture, and to keep

Its victim still alive, and quivering;

And, with it paragoned, why canker is

An angel of compassion!   Yet against grief

What boots it to rebel?   It is the shadow

Which still accompanies our sun of joy;

And, when the shadow blots out all the shine,

I fall not unto railing, but, forlorn,

I steep my soul in silence, and I pray.

ARAN.

Pray!   I am weary of the word.   Why pray,

When never an answer cometh to our prayer?

Have we not prayed, we, and our sires, and, so,

Their sires, for lives on miserable lives,

Burning the flesh of goats, the fat of kine,

And, sacrificing yeanlings when our dams

Were smit with barrenness; yielding our last

In the vain hope still to propitiate

The Power that took our first?   I am sick of prayer!

When did prayer keep the murrain from our herds,
Or once avert the vultures? Have our flocks
More teeming wombs, thicker or softer fleece?
Or doth the sprouting soil no longer crack
For lack of moisture, stubbornly denied,
That in untimely torrents it may swoop
On the slow-ripening grain, and beat it flat?
These are the fruits of prayer. We pray, while He
Hideth aloft in churlish majesty,
Rolling His wanton thunder overhead,
And splitting with His lightning, flashed for sport,
The trunk that gave us shelter. No! the hour
For prayer is past; the hour for deeds is here,
Whose stroke shall render prayer superfluous.

NOEMA.

Alas! you do not heed me. But one boon,
One last, one only boon, I yet would urge.
Oh! leave at least to piety and me
The tender, dark-eyed darling of my womb.
Leave me my Irad! Him you cannot need,
Nor he promote your direful strategy.
He is so young, so helpless, and so dear.
'Twas my long-suffering womb that fostered him;

Sheltered his yet sheathed senses from all hurt,
And fed him with the rain of my life's blood.
Who was it communed with him, while as yet
His life was dim and shapeless as a dream?
Who opened to the light his pretty cheeks,
And kissed his eyelids into consciousness?
Taught him your name? moulded his little lips
Into a filial welcome?   Who but I?
And when enlarging thought could apprehend
The august sense of father, I it was
Who did project your image into Heaven,
And told him of another Father there.
Oh! how would you be patient if one came
'Twixt you and him, and spurred him to rebel
Against your sceptre and authority?
Nay, make him not a rebel,—for my sake!
I have lain nights awake to give him sleep;
And——

ARAN.

Be it as you will.   He is a child,
And you a woman: ye are fairly yoked.
And both will reap the harvest of our act,
Who would not sow the seed.   Now, to our meal.

NOEMA.

Had you come timelier to-night, we might
Have entertained an unaccustomed guest.
A Spirit from I know not where, but clad
In garb of airy beauty, settled here,
Just after sunset.

ARAN.

Spake he of the Tower?

NOEMA.

No syllable.   But he discoursed so sweetly
Of Earth, and stars, and all that moves between,—
I would that you had heard him.

ARAN.

I have no stomach for such windy food.
I feared perchance he hither came to balk,
Celestial marplot, our terrestrial plans,
Sent by the Arch-designer of our doom.
But if he only fooled you with fresh dreams,
Foibles and follies of your woman's breast;
It touches me but little ; and I yield.
Monopoly of such a guest to one,
Who is a fitting hostess.   Food, now, food !

[ARAN goes in.   NOEMA lingers a while without.

NOEMA (*alone*).

Because I am a woman! Is it then
So small a thing? Just large enough for man
To see and step aside from, lest he crush!
Yet what can crush worse than indifference,
Or that misplaced compassion which denies
All common kinship? Yon superior Spirit
Disowned me not, but wished that he were man,
Because I am a woman. That was a note
Showed him attuned to heavenly harmony.
Oh! with what nectared yet decorous words
Did he extol me,—almost as though he loved!
Yet 'twas not love which made that Spirit deem
My plain defects perfection, but, perchance,
That spiritual insight which perceives
Imperfect nought, leaving to lower man
To find things faulty through his faultiness.
This very Earth which we so oft reproach,
He lauded likewise, though his tenderest tones,
I own, were kept for me. Yet, yet, 'tis sure
Love it was not. It were impossible
Spirit should be enamoured of the flesh,
And in the glamour of his far-off home,

He will forget me, and will come no more.

That were a loss indeed to leave life blank,

And make to-morrow dead as yesterday.

Yet, he *will* come.   He said he would; and I

Bade not adieu, but welcome, when he went.

To love a Spirit, surely were not sin!

Can it be wrong to love—wings and a voice?

And were I with him now, what could befall,

Or fare between us there, to derogate

From carnal homage still exacted here,

And given, if all unwillingly?   Ay, there it is!

True love makes false love loathing, and one hour

Of spiritual intercourse bequeaths

A life of shrinking from terrestrial lips.

And I must sleep in Aran's arms to-night!

END OF ACT I

D

ACT II

SCENE I

Early morning, a week later than Act I.   The sun not yet
risen, but red rays shooting upward from the eastern
horizon into a cloudless and sultry sky.   The plain of
Shinar, from which the first massive storeys of the
Tower arise in slowly narrowing spirals.   Gangs of male
bondmen ascending and descending, carrying slime and
bricks.   Groups of women mixing slime.

ARAN, SIDON, EBER, KORAH, PELEG.   Crowd of Freemen.

MALE BONDMEN (*chanting*).

Faster, faster, ever faster,
Moves our weary-circling labour,
While the stern and strong taskmaster
Drives us on with thong and sabre.
Resting but refreshens sorrow,
Slumber keeps our bondage endless ;

Time forgets us, and to-morrow,
Like to-day, beholds us friendless.

                 Faster—Faster !

CHORUS OF WOMEN.

In anguish and wailing
    Our babes see the light,
Drenched with tears unavailing
    As cries in the night.
In the womb we but cherish
    A victim, a slave ;
Born to suffer, then perish,
    And sleep in the grave.

MALE SLAVES (*chanting*).

Sweating, straining, panting, bleeding,
    Upward, storey piled on storey,
Climb we still, for lords unheeding
    Aught save ease, and gain, and glory.
We are of the self-same leaven ;
    They, as we, are sad and mortal ;
Yet if we did win them Heaven,
    They would leave us at the portal,

                 Bleeding, panting !

CHORUS OF WOMEN.

Pile the bricks, mix the mortar;
　　The blinder we plod,
Life will seem to us shorter,
　　Less pitiless, God.
The sooner the levin
　　Of death will descend,
And the harshness of Heaven
　　And Earth have an end.

ARAN.

With what a fervent and continuous will
They seem to work, this morn, as though the fire
Of our great undertaking had infected
Even their sluggish and inferior veins.
Such is the virtue of high enterprise.
It drags along with it, as to the goal,
The wheels that bear it thither.　Sorry dupes !
Did ye hear their song?　They fain would have us
　　deem
They count upon no harvest for their toil,
And are but sickles blunted in our hand
By act of reaping.　But I know them well.

The feeble ever still dissimulate,

And with a cunning feint creep underneath

The blundering thrust of strength.   'Tis their redress.

But in their hearts they hopeful rebels are,

Setting no brick of this stupendous Tower,

But that they think to frame our sepulchre,

And their redemption.   We must baffle them.

As we to Heaven, so unto us they stand,

And 'twere a barren issue of our work,

To dethrone God, were we ourselves dethroned.

KORAH.

There spake the tyrant and the slave at once.

What ! you would hack your gyves off, but to clamp

Their teeth upon another : strain at power,

Only to keep your fellows powerless,

And from the clutch of the gangmaster's hand

Wrench the keen whip that seams and scores your
  flesh,

To flog your brother with !   Most villainous !

If this but be the purport of our Tower,

May swift the rampant lightning smite its top,

And following thunder shake its selfish base,

And bury us beneath it !

ARAN.

Hark to him !

This is the folly we can hear at home,
Babbled by lips of women.   See you not
Some one must serve? and to emancipate
All equally, would only render thrall
All men alike.   If we should mend our lot,
Theirs may be mended too; withal, there must
'Twixt us and them be due discrepancy.
The very secret of the sky, we seek
By our assault to learn, is how to rule,
And keep weak spirits in subjection;
And though, when once triumphant, we might be
More merciful than it, our mercy would
Not plan our own effectual overthrow.
Thank Heaven for this at least, it hath not made
All men mere maunderers.

KORAH.

No, nor all men blind.

You bid me look; 'tis you that cannot see.
You are the dreamer, if you think to keep
The solace of fermenting discontent
From the bare hearth of hungry-trudging toil.
There is it most at home; not 'neath the roof

Of purple pomp and roomy luxury :
And, could you drive it from the proud man's gate,
'Twould refuge take in hovels of the poor.
'Tis the one guest that's entertained by all,
The uncomfortable comfort of our lives,
Though welcome not, yet never sent away,
To-morrow's promised balance 'gainst to-day.
It is our common brotherhood that breeds
Common dissatisfaction with our lot ;
And common brotherhood should bid us seek
A common remedy, to heal us all.
Ay, build your Tower, and pluck you down the skies
From their unpitying proud pre-eminence ;
But, having purged the Heavens of their pride,
Keep not the foul distemper for the Earth.
Yes, I believe the time will come when men
Will be as free and equal as the waves,
That seem to jostle but that never jar,
Which climb and sink together, interfuse,
Grow smooth with meeting, interchange their shapes,
And in each other merge identity.
Blest be the aspirations of the Tower,
Hastening the advent of that day !   If not,
A thousand curses on it !

SIDON.

Well said, both.

But well said is not wisdom.   Sense and sound
But rarely travel coupled.   Life, large life,
Cannot be wrapped in phrases ; they are too small.
And when of life we would neat parcels make,
Just as we stop one end with reasons, it
Runs out on t'other side.   As for yon Tower,
'Tis a tall toy, made for the Gods to play with.
For Gods are many or none.   Beyond your God,
Either there dwells another, godlier,
Or, like ourselves, they wrangle and dispute,
And half their blows descend upon our heads ;
And from their harmony we suffer more
Even than from their discord.   They agree,
Their strifes suspended, to make sport of us,
Treating us much as boys treat cockroaches :
They prick us just to see what we will do.
Shrink, and they prick us more, to know what next.
But case yourselves in mailed indifference,
They fancy you inanimate or dead,
And leave you to your numbness.   There's the cure !
'Tis patience makes us level with the Gods,
And baffles their malignity.   In vain

The thong is plied on him who will not yield
One cry to cheer the scourger. That is a Tower,
Which needs no building, and is never o'erthrown.

PELEG.

And this is called divine philosophy,
That thinks to outwit God ! Patience is well,
But not because man's burden may not be
Shifted or lightened ever, but that the hand
Which doth impose it is a hand all-wise,
The back that bears it, foolish. Sacrifice,
Prayer, and first fruits, can still propitiate
The Being whom insurrection will not move.
Man's lot is hard, do you say ? How do we know,
It were not harder yet, did we not proffer
Frankincense and the fragrant steam of flesh,
Entrails and caul of calves, rams without stain,
She-goats, and morn and evening holocaust ?
With these we keep the thunder in the skies,
The ocean in its bed, which else would mount
And roll a final deluge o'er the Earth.
Pile high the Tower; but, when its top is crowned,
To Heaven its whorls ascending dedicate,

And Heaven perchance will condescend to lift
Some feathers of your fardel.

EBER.

Worthy priest,
While you among the bowels of the slain
Have still been pottering, or devoutly bent
Over the blood of writhing turtle-doves,
I through the silent watches of the night
Have scanned the long procession of the stars,
In even courses moving ; caught the rhythm
Of the melodious planets as they chime,
Each after each, over the measured sky.
And I have marked that in that upper world
There is continuous concord, order firm,
And a most noble discipline. The clouds
Are fitful, seeing they are born of earth ;
But beyond our capricious envelope
Abides a steady sphere, serene of will,
And governed by a sovran certainty.
I chide no living heart that strives and soars,
And it may be this pile magnificent
Will yield to Aran all he hopes from it,
And unto those who build it. But, for me,

I watch with joy its scaling spirals rise,

Since by its growing summit I am taken

Nearer and nearer to the orbs that are

The alphabet of knowledge, whence I seek

To shape a language that shall speak to all

Of what they need to learn : how to conform

To method never wavering, and provide

Against vicissitudes no human power

Can hope to avert, but still to be foreseen :

So that no second deluge find us bare

Of arks of shelter.   Stars will teach us this,

And not libations.   Yours is the one void task ;

For nought is wholly impotent save prayer.

ARAN.

Well ended at the least !   I did not think

That an astrologer could be so wise.

You have learned somewhat from your star-gazing.

Henceforward are you welcome to a post

Upon our topmost balcony, to watch

The womanish mutations of the moon.

There, perched 'twixt earth and sky, you chance may
        catch

Some whispers of the jealous firmament,

And pass them on to us; playing the part
Of daring eavesdropper, under the roof of Heaven.
You cannot mar our work, and you may aid it.
But not with Peleg's tactics do I hold,
Nor yet with Sidon's; for, in scales of sense,
I find an even balance 'tween the Priest
And the Philosopher, in whom there is
A common emptiness.   How say ye, friends?

THE CROWD.

We say with Aran.   Long live Aran! long
May solid counsel, kin to his, prevail!

ARAN.

We are not *all* philosophers; we are men.

THE CROWD.

True, we are men, and not philosophers!
That should make Sidon wince.

ARAN.

                 And we, being men,
Men, and not worms more than philosophers,
Will not be trodden on by men or Gods.
As for poor Korah's unripe fantasies,

I put it to you, friends!   Will you consent
That slave and free shall ever be confused,
Or that the menial myriads you behold
Swarming about that goodly scaffolding,
Shall with you share dominion and delight?
'Tis in the Tower that our salvation hides ;
But what we claim from Heaven is comely life,
Comely and pleasant ; mastery over Fate,
The government of rain and wind and drouth,
Harvest abounding, honey, and wine, and oil ;
Fat flocks, and herds unvisited by pest,
No fever, ache, nor ague, but an Earth
Fixed and serene as Eber's vaunted spheres,
Long jocund days, and nights in rapture steeped,
Submissive wives, children as dense as bloom,
And ample store of docile concubines.
We ask no more ; but these are what we ask.

THE CROWD.

Nought beyond these.   And if we them obtain,
Aran's blest name shall through the ages live !

ARAN.

Then let us urge them faster.   Each to his post,

And there accelerate the lagging hour,

When the usurping Deity shall hear

Our thunder at His gates, and His high throne

Fall with a clash to the abyss of Hell !

CHORUS OF WOMEN (*chanting*).

In anguish and wailing
Our babes see the light,
Drenched with tears unavailing
As cries in the night.
In the womb we but cherish
A victim, a slave ;
Born to suffer, then perish,
And sleep in the grave !

SCENE II

The tents of ARAN.   Same morning and hour as in Scene I.
The topmost circles of the Tower visible in the distance,
with Ararat beyond.   NOEMA.   IRAD.

IRAD.

Dear mother, let me go !   I see the Tower

Rising and rising higher and higher each day ;

And, every morn I wake, I can descry
More and still more of its great head.   What harm
To see it near, more than to see it far?

NOEMA.

Would that you could not see it, far or near.
It is a thing accurst, and, some dread morn
Or angry night, will topple down and be
For its projectors grave and monument.
What, Irad, if you stood beneath it then?

IRAD.

I am not frightened, mother.

NOEMA.

                            Would that you were!
But, in the breast of each male whelp that breathes,
There lurks a devilish audacity,
Which stamps on Earth, and brandishes its pride
Against the face of Heaven.   Times, I think,
Not Adam surely, but fell Lucifer,
Was the first father of the race, and left
His rebel poison in the womb of Eve,
To taint all later sons.   In vain our meek

And trembling dispositions do conceive,
Foster, and suckle them.   Our daughters take
The impress of their mother; but our boys,
Since cast in the superb Archangel's die,
Consort with terror !

IRAD.

Then I will not go.
Nay, weep not, mother.   I will sail my boat
Upon the shallows by the river brink,
Returning to you shortly.

NOEMA.

Kiss me, Irad !
For, if you feel the male ferocity,
You have the true male gentleness as well
Thus should it be.   The noblest men still are
Tough as the bole, but tender as the leaves ;
And, while the strangling hurricane in vain
Writhes round their trunk, one little tearful cloud
Or kissing zephyr stirs their foliage.
Go to the river, then ; but, Irad, heed
That you still keep the shallows.

SCENE III

NOEMA.

                               I am alone,
Alone, as long I wished.   Yet do I wish
Wholly to be alone?   I cannot say it.
Oh ! where is He, that shadow of myself,
Which I project, or as I sit or move,
And, shadow-like, is still before, behind,
But never quite beside me !   Yesterday,
Leagued with to-morrow, kills the day that is,
And life subsists on memory and hope.
Was it a dream ?   Hath he forgotten me ?
Or have the envious Heavens snatched him back,
And clipped his too erratic pinions ?
Was it a dream, only a dream ?   But no !
I saw his fair celestial properties,
Heard his articulate distinctive voice,
And felt his airy aromatic wings
Swaying above me as he breathed farewell.
Was that a dream, then all the world's a dream,
Yon upstart spirals wreaths of rising mist,

E

The mountains flimsy as the atmosphere,

The sun himself an ignus-fatuus,

And all our senses only visionary.

It was no dream; it is the waking seems so.

Oh! shall I never gaze upon him more,

And must the sweetness of that single hour

Be long life's lasting bitterness? I feel

No wish to name him now; only to hide

The tumult he has bred! I sometimes think

That when we lock a secret in our breast,

True to its task, that soft recess assumes

The casket's hardness. O how hard mine feels!

Hark!

A VOICE SINGING.

Over the realms of balsam and of myrrh,
I have flown, I have flown,
And endless deserts plumed with snow and fir,
All alone, all alone,
Seeing if other on the Earth there were,
Like my own, like my own!

NOEMA.

It is His voice! I could distinguish it

Were all the Heavens singing at the time.
'Tis in the air, and yet I cannot see him.

Under the date-palms fringing tropic lakes,
I have lain, I have lain,
And icy caves, where Winter never wakes
From its pain, from its pain:
O for that region which my pinion aches
To regain, to regain!

NOEMA.

But why are you invisible? I hear
Your silvery notes, yet fail to find the spot
Where you hang poising.

AFRAEL.

I am on the ground,
Not in the air, and full in front of you.
It must be daylight dazzles you, and that
Spirits resemble sunshine, and the form,
You in the gloaming plainly could discern,
Is now confounded with the garish day.
But look! look! here,—here where I bend o'er you!

NOEMA (*shading her eyes.*)

Ha! I surmise you now, and, as I gaze,
Do from the ambient sunshine round you off,
And recognise your seeming.   But, how bright,
Wondrously bright you glow, and, while the air
Shimmers unstably, you serenely shine.
Whence have you come so early in the hours?

AFRAEL.

Straight from my star, the star of dark and dawn.
I met a lark, hieing to heaven, and shaking
Dew from his feet and music from his wings,
And I did ask him of thee.   At the which,
He shrilled out such a volume of sweet sound,
It filled the azure-vaulted firmament,
And set the stars a-ringing.   Then I knew
He from the heaven below, where thou dost dwell,
Had plumed his flight; and through the air I slid,
Adown the path by which he had ascended.
Lo! he hath proved to me a trusty guide,
And happy be his song amid the clouds!

NOEMA.

My blessing, too, go with that messenger!

For I did think never to see you more ;
But, like a bird that on the topmost spray
Of some dark solitary tree alights,
Only to shake it with its song, then leave,
That you had perched an instant on my life,
To make it lonely ever afterward !

AFRAEL.

How couldst think that, when still my wings kept
    warm
The sense of that brief tenancy, and yearned
To close once more on their delicious perch ?
O that I were a nightingale, that I
Might hide within the scented coppice nigh
The curtain of the chamber where thou keepest,
And with my song accompany thy dreams !
Be that, be anything but what I am,
Since what I am keeps me so far from thee !

NOEMA.

Why did you bridle your return so long,
And with delay torture expectancy ?

AFRAEL.

When, in the dwindling twilight of that eve

Consumed in happy intercourse, I sailed
Back to my native ether, I conceived
A pang at parting never felt before,
Parting from whence I might ; for novelty
Hath ever been, and is, the Spirit's joy.
But, from the hour when I my pinions fledged
To quit thee, novelty had lost its charm.
There was no sun in heaven, no room in space,
No freshness in infinity, nothing new
In all the illimitable realms of air.
Then had I winged to thee, direct, when lo !
A strange surmise arrested my descent.
What if it were the quality of Earth
To tame the pulse of Spirits, and compel
Him who hath once its narrow bounds essayed,
Still to return, and if it was not Thou,
But the mere planet's self, which had subdued
The once discursive temper of my flight ?
Swift through the intervening air I shot,
And on the Earth alighted, but not here.
Mountains magnificent, and inland seas,
Forests of trunks stupendous, sweeping heaven
With dark audacious tops, snow-fed cascades,
Taking anon the whiteness of their birth,

Then flashing into silver; oceans vast
With endless manes uplifted, foam-lashed strands,
Sweet-watered valleys, cool, and ever green,
Darkling ravines o'er-pent by crags that faced
And frowned against each other; waving meads
By asphodel and amaranth o'errun,
Stirred into music by the soughing breeze;
Lands of wide ribless snow and strident winds,
And howled at by the hungry hurricanes;
Realms of rank heat, and then of scorching cold,
And middle zones of genial compromise
Betwixt these fierce extremes;—o'er these, o'er all,
O'er many more I sailed with curious wing,
Skimming the uneven globe, its heights, its depths,
My fragile self to it surrendering,
That it might make me subject to its power.
Then to the heaven of heavens I backward soared,—
Seven times the sun having withdrawn his light,
The while I journeyed o'er the earth,—and there
Myself replenished with celestial food.

NOEMA.

But did you in your travel hap on none
Like unto us? no man, no woman,——

AFRAEL.

None,
Though life abounded. In the deep-troughed waves,
Grim monsters rolled and belched. By river-banks
Mountainous creatures basked, their bulging backs
Cracked by the sun. In jungles choked with growth
And knotted stems, prowled gloomy-visaged beasts,
Savage though beautiful, and, as I passed,
Snapped at my wings; others, as meek as fair,
Halted and glanced, then, twinkling, disappeared
In leafy coverts; many-plumaged birds,
Dovelike and gentle, piping to themselves,
Amid a world of sportive butterflies.
But nowhere found I trace of aught like thee,
Or those thou callest thine, though all seemed fit
To be their dwelling : only mute expanse
Of hills, and woods, and wastes, and grievous seas
Moaning around unpeopled continents.

NOEMA.

O would that Aran had been here, to hark
This wondrous tale, and therefrom learn what home,
What Heaven, we have to master, and desist
From vain aggression on the foreign sky !

But did you mark the egregious edifice
Which yonder looms upon the horizon big,
And with still growingly aggressive gaze
Threatens the firmament?

AFRAEL.

What may it be?

NOEMA.

An engine of presumption reared by man
To wreck his God; a ladder by whose rungs
Would climbing mortals the Immortal reach,
And hurl Him to its base; Tower from whose top
Earth is to spring and find itself in Heaven.

AFRAEL.

Why doth not Earth content Earth's denizens,
And eyes that see begrudge the Invisible
Its shroud of darkness?

NOEMA.

Ah! because 'tis Earth,
And what men see, and see not, are confused
In a perpetual twilight.   Do you not know
The melancholy story of our race?

AFRAEL.

No.   Gladly would I learn it from thy lips.

NOEMA.

There was a garden paradise where roamed
A man and woman, parent of us all,
Though not like us degenerate, but he
Comely as thou, she far more fair than I.

. AFRAEL.

O would that thou and I had been that pair,
And were it still !

NOEMA.

                    Happy indeed they were,
As you too fondly deem we too should be,
So circumstanced : not happy to the end.
For in the Garden one strange Tree there bloomed,
One only, of the which they might not eat,—
For God forbade,—the Tree whose fruit conferred
Knowledge of Good and Evil.   But they ate.
Straightway the veil of innocence was rent,
And mirrored in each other's minds they saw
The base-born brood of Self; greedy desire,

Grudges, and petulance, and secret aims,
Anger, remorse, reciprocal reproach,
And they who hitherto had been but one,
Were two henceforth.

AFRAEL.

Was there no remedy?

NOEMA.

'Tis said there was. There stood another tree,
The Tree of Life, of which had they but plucked,—
Such is the tale obscure tradition tells,—
They might have lived for ever, and so balked
The doom which fell upon them, doom of death.
But ere that dismal fault could be repaired,
God drove them from the Garden, and, its gates
Guarding with sword of flaming cherubim,
Propelled them to the wilderness, where toil
Is each one's heritage, and tares, and thorns,
Emblems of direr grief, mix with the corn
Raised by the sweat and furrows of the brow.

AFRAEL.

But is toil pain? Is it but energy,
The same delicious hurricane of will

That sends me thridding in and out the stars,
Bore me around this deep-indented globe,
And brings me to thy feet ?   Such toil is rapture !

NOEMA.

Yes, for such toil hath pleasure for its end,
Not profit, and involves none other's pain ;
Whereas all mortal energy may fail,
And toil like ours means jarring interests,
And is as though in the unfrontiered air
The wingëd tenants of your star should clash,
Because their rival pinions strove to beat
The self-same pathway.

AFRAEL.

           That we never do.
For Spirits, when they meet, oft lightning make,
But never, thunder.

NOEMA.

         So !   That tells me why
On summer nights I see the flashes play
About the horizon, though the skies be clear,
And all the stars lustrous and imminent.

Would it were so with us ! But we, alas !
Circling in narrow rounds, for ever cross
Each other's track, then push for mastery.
For man hath still a double war to wage,
War against Nature, and thence war with man.
One brings the body ache and age, and one
Bequeaths the heart disgust, despondency,
And hatred of that Self for which, despite
That very hate, we still are forced to strive.

AFRAEL.

Strange tale, that sounds like truth, if I surmise
Rightly its import.   What might be the fruit,
The seed of so much bane, or wherefore He,
Who put it in their way, forbade its use,
Outsoars conjecture ; for, to us no less,
Beyond is still the portal of Beyond,
And Cause is lost in links of Consequence.
This much, withal, seems plain : your ancestors,
Touching a tree forbidden them, exchanged
Forthwith a prosperous will for needy want,
And, in the place of careless appetites
Which found immediate banquet, there arose
Necessity for labour, forethought, greed,

And fears anent the Future.   Thence I see
How Self was first begotten,—dismal Self,
Which pines within the dungeon that it builds,
Deeming therein is sole security.
But is there no escape from Self, no rift
In the chill cloud Self's self doth generate,
Through which Unself shines visible beyond?

NOEMA.

O yes, there is! though it be transitory.
Amid this bare flat desert of our lives,
Through whose deep sand with staggering feet we plod,
Its heat, its drouth, its length, its weariness,
With still the same horizon, lo! sometimes
A green oasis shimmers.   Oft it proves
Only a mirage, and the saddened heart,
Whose credulous pulse had quickened at the cheat,
Back to its old monotony subsides,
And beats the minutes idly.   Oh! but when
It is no mirage, no distressful lie,
The desert is forgotten, life and death,
And all the loathsome loads betwixt the twain
We bear, poor wretched sumpters!   Then we halt,
Unpack each other's fardels, bending see

Each other's face reflected in the wave,
Drink from the self-same fount, and make our couch
Under the self-same starlit canopy !

AFRAEL.

And what is this oasis ?

NOEMA.

It is Love.

AFRAEL.

And what is Love ?

NOEMA.

Love ? Love is what it is !
Like nothing else in all the universe,
So is there nought it can be likened to.
To those who know it, patent, but to those
Who ne'er have known.it, indescribable.
Go tell me what the tree feels, when in spring
The sweet insidious sap begins to stir
About its roots, flushes the stagnant rind,
And through the gnarled and gouty trunk transmits
The genial shock, till every limb and branch

Thrills to the spray-tips : what the mountain stream,
When glittering April uncongeals its bed,
And sends it dancing downward to the vale,
Singing the songs of wayward liberty :
Or what the Night must feel, when the deep dark,
Which is but secret seeing, veils the Earth,
And the bare breast of hushed Heaven throbs with
    stars !
Tell me all these, and I will tell you then
What the distinctions and delights of Love.
'Tis a fifth season, a sixth sense, a light,
A warmth beyond the cunning of the sun ;
Another element ; fire, water, air,
Nor burn, nor quench, nor feed it, for it lives
Steeped in its self-provided atmosphere !

AFRAEL.

You make me feel like liberated stream,
Like the warm trunk, like to the trancëd night,
And all the spheres of all the firmament
Seem to lack something now !   Still, how doth
    Love
Baffle that self, which dimly I discern
Is Earth's essential bane ?

NOEMA.

Because it is

A transcendental egotism, Love,—

Which deifies a dearer self, and makes

The heart a shrine, pure for the sake of it;

Upon whose altar Self by self is slain,

And adoration crowned by sacrifice.

Love dwelleth in the tents of the beloved,

Though countless leagues of pasture intervene.

Its thoughts, its wants, are otherwhere ; time, space,

And all conventions, are its enemies.

It sickens for one only voice; the note

Of viol, flute, and hollowed instrument,

Untuned by that, remains unmusical,

Or but delivers discord.   Such is Love ;

And they whose stagnant spirits have been stirred

Once by its subterranean current, know

That Love is all, and all beside is nought,

Emptiness, and the ticking of the brain !

AFRAEL.

Why, then, I love thee !   For that spreading dome

Of boundless blue, which round the universe

Nor endeth nor beginneth, and whose orbs

F

Are countless as its uncontainéd leagues,
Within whose inexhaustible expanse,
Which knoweth no Without, my pinions range
As unconditioned as itself, and find
Endless pursuit, endless variety,—
Since in that tender twilight I alit
Upon this new-found sphere, and felt my wings
Ruffled with unknown rapture,—hath but seemed
Infinite void, infinite weariness,
And purposeless distraction !   Here alone,
Here in the palm-trees' shade, this spot of Earth,
To which by mortal chances thou art fixed,
Do I now find station and amplitude.
There is no pleasant pathway through the stars,
Save toward this bourne it bends ; no journeying,
Which doth not tire before it doth begin,
Unless it doth propose thee for its end.
Thou fillest for me the spacious universe,
And art its centre, and circumference too !
Say, is this love ?

NOEMA.

'Tis strangely like to it !
But mortal love, though mortals' benison,

Would to immortals surely be but bane.

Love, that can lift us half-way to the spheres,

Must, if thou couldst subserve its influence,

Lure thee half-way below them.   Thou art a Spirit ;

And Love, for all its potent witchery,

Inextricably tangled in the flesh,

Could not strike root in thee.   O, man is gross,

And even his finest motions sensibly

From the affections of the body start,

Or feebly flag towards it as their goal.

That is the final tragedy of all,

When Love immortal dies !   When two fair beings,

Who were the morning in each other's eyes,

Fade into irrecoverable night,

And hear each other through the darkness call,

But never find each other's faces more !

AFRAEL.

Why doth it close like that ?   Is it because

Flesh is the edge of that catastrophe,

And rash Love topples over ?   I were safe

From such a precipice, for Spirit walks

Along the crest of all things, undismayed,

Nor ever dizzied by sheer eminence.

My love for thee,—for let me call it love,
If only that the word sounds heavenly sweet,—
Would be as long-enduring as myself,
Who cannot end.

NOEMA.

O to be loved by a Spirit, and for ever !
What could a woman dream of more than that ?

AFRAEL.

Then let me love !

NOEMA.

     How can I hinder you,
So that you love ?

AFRAEL.

Within my wings will I enfold my love,
And bear it with me to the firmament,
And through the envious constellations sail
With my new treasure for companion !
But will not thou thyself, source of this love,
Lend thy divine attractions to my flight,
And let me cleave for thee with feathery plumes
The all too dense and opaque envelope

That wraps thy earthly habitation round,

And buoy thee up through heavenly distances,

Whose distance ne'er will lessen, since its goal,

A canopy of ether that is hung

Over our heads, will with our soaring soar?

Say me but yes, and come with me this night,

When to thy seeming all the stars will wake,

Though sleep ne'er comes to their unwearied orbs!

NOEMA.

Mean you that I should quit the kindred ground,

And with you journey through the alien air?

I, all of flesh compounded, should be borne

Upon the supersensuous elements,

And this my carnal weight be lifted up

Along with one, lightsome and volatile?

AFRAEL.

Yes, that is what I ask.

NOEMA.

                    Then, then indeed,

Indeed you love me! love alone could shape

A dream so airy and fantastical.

AFRAEL.

Let me but once my Spirit's force essay
On thy fair matter, when the winds are still,
And the down-hanging curtains of the night
Are diapered with stars? this night, this night,
The one that's nearest!

NOEMA.

A woman's nights are mostly servitude,
But this one lifts the yoke.　There will be held
A mid-nocturnal parley at the Tower,
And I shall watch alone, while Irad floats
With dreamy sails o'er sleep's soft-heaving sea.
Come, then, to-night!

AFRAEL.

　　　　　　Yes, I to-night will come.
But may meanwhile the love, which here I lay
Soft on thy breast, like water-lily sink
Into the depths that give it sustenance!

　　　　　　　　[AFRAEL ascends into the air.

NOEMA (*alone*).

I cannot choose but love him.　Love him?　No!

But let myself be loved.   That's different,

And may not be escaped by willing it.

And even to love a Spirit were no more

Than being enamoured of the atmosphere,

The glitter of the morning, or the strain

Of joyous bird deep-hidden in the brake ;

While to be loved by Spirit, were to have

A suitor less familiar than the wind,

Who kisses brow and cheek, and asks no leave.

Still, Love, for all our reasoning, retains

Such arguments to swift confound our words,

That they who know him best, know likewise this,

To name him is to tremble. . . . Oh ! I trust,

He will not come to-night !

SCENE IV

EBER and IRAD approach.   IRAD runs forward to his mother.

IRAD.

See ! mother ! mother !

See what a ship Eber has made for me !

The keel is carved from cedar-wood, the prow

Is beaked and curled, the hull is hollowed out,

And holds a cargo of the richest dates,
We plucked together.   From the canes that grow,—
You know them, mother,—on the Euphrates' banks,
He cut these great tall masts, and from their leaves,
Hauled from the water, shaped the flapping sails.
The cordage is of palm-pith, and the crew
Moulded from river-slime.   They are at work,
Tug at the ropes, feel at the helm, and sit
Among the shrouds like living mariners.
Is it not wonderful?

> [EBER comes up.

NOEMA.

                    A mother's thanks
That you have so much kindliness to waste
Upon her child.

IRAD.

                    When will you take me, Eber?

NOEMA.

Tax Eber now no more with your demands,
But with your silence pay your gratitude.
Take your ship, Irad, your magnificent ship,
And find it storage among dwarfer boats.

IRAD.

But see the name Eber has burnt on it !
The Tower! The Tower! My ship is called The Tower!
Why, everybody loves the Tower but mother,
But chiding, darling mother.

> [He throws his arms round NOEMA and kisses her.

Now I go,
To find my ship a good dry landing-place.
Again, I thank you, Eber,—thank you, thank you !

> [Exit.

NOEMA.

I wish you had not called his toy The Tower.
The name is hateful.

EBER.

What is there to hate ?
It is a toy like Irad's : bigger truly,
As are its builders ; but a toy at which
The Gods but smile, even as we smile at his.

NOEMA.

Why do you speak of Gods ? There is one God,
Tradition tells, one only, one in Heaven.

EBER.

Tradition is a senile counsellor,
With memory half gone.   The same old tales
She loves to mumble, and distort afresh.
She is a toothless crone, whose jumbling wit
Ranges through gossip, dreams, fears, tattered scraps
Of musty prophecy, report, surmise,
And quick-grown rumour, which when pierced, betrays,
Like to a specious spurious agaric,
But smoke and stench inside.   Tradition chokes
Discovery's highway, nor can single truth
Elbow its road through fable's dense-packed crowd.
Gods there may be, or God ; 'tis yet to prove.
Perchance we ne'er shall prove it.   But 'tis well
To clinch this on the mind,—that oft there hides
A treasure-trove even in old women's tales,
Though, like a rubbish-heap, they scarcely tempt
A nice hand to disturb them.

NOEMA.

          I am a woman ;
And likely we are all,—old, young, and those
Nor young nor old,—to wisdom foolishness.

Yet, may be, ever and anon we have
Glimpses of things too coy to let the wise
On their mysterious delicacy stare.
But tell me, what is doing at the Tower;
If Aran wields authority as sure
As when he first affirmed it?

EBER.

More, far more.
Rebellion stooped to pick up brands this morn,
But quick he snatched them from its half-raised
    arm,
And smote its back with its own instruments.
O, it was rare to see the front with which
He frowned down Korah, and the flashing eyes
Before whose scorching fire even Peleg shrank,
Lest it should blister him.   For though I rate
Their Tower but as a ladder whence I may,
Deciphering, read Heaven's starry hieroglyphs,
Male courage in the male breast echo wakes,
And, like an instant hurricane that straight
Tears out the heart o' the forest with its teeth,
He carried all before him.   Long live Aran!

Long live our liberation ! loudly rang
Up all the massive whorls of the huge Tower,
That seemed to shake with shouting.

NOEMA.

And the end ?

EBER.

I am nor prophet nor priest ; and he who scans
The certain skies, learns to be diffident
Of what is all uncertain.   But of late
Have I marked strange conjunctions which, if read
With due intelligence, to portents point :
Convulsion in the top and bottom worlds,
With trouble in their middle atmospheres ;
Quakes, tremors, tempests, tides irregular,
All order topsy-turvy, ordered yet
By supereminent Order which defies
The reach of calculation short as mine.

NOEMA.

But have you not warned Aran of these portents ?

EBER.

Warned Aran! 'Twere as sane to warn the wave
It will against the shore be splintered spray,
Warn the fierce-grinning tiger, ere it spring,
It will but leap upon the hunter's spear,
As Aran warn with message from the sky.
His road towards Heaven, and mine, are different,
And I should tack and trim where he sails slap
In the gale's brunt.   But 'tis a fearless heart.
And fearlessness, accounted much by men,
Sums conquest over women.   Fare you well!

[Exit.

NOEMA (*alone*).

But why should we be conquered?   Why not won
With patient arts of gentle mastery?
We are crushed easily; that's sure enough.
But is it well or wise, manly or just,
To plant the heel of domination down
With such an emphasis on things so soft?
For we are less than they, more subtle, weak,
Unstable, more the clouds of accident;
And only that perverseness, which is part
Of our infirmity, would claim a place

Of equal sway beside them.   Like control
Begets a like responsibility ;
And Heaven forbid that we should ever be
Responsible against the storms, rebuffs,
And rude surprises of the world, that would
O'erwhelm us utterly !   We need a shield,
But shield which, rough upon the foeful side,
Wears yet a smooth concavity, nor galls
The following breast, it has to save from hurt.
If fearlessness were all, why then one might
As well go couple with the hugging bear,
Lie with the pard and suckle his hot cubs,
Be littered with the lion, kiss the wolf,
Or feel the scratching of the tiger's claws
Upon one's back in amorous savagery.
O gentle-touching Spirit ! *thou* dost not crush,
Nor make me feel my inequality,
Though betwixt thee and me extends the space
That lies 'twixt Earth and Heaven.   I to thee
Could live subservient ever, and look up
As fondly as at some indifferent star,
Seen through blue rifts of fleecy-flying clouds.
Yet in thy star remain, nor answer me
With the fulfilment of my timid wants,

Which, if they saw the long-feigned goal too near,
Would turn and run affrighted, to regain
The safe confinement of their starting-place.
Such contradiction fights in woman's veins.
He must not come to-night!

END OF ACT II

ACT III

SCENE I

Night of the same day.   Interior of the chief tent of ARAN.
NOEMA.   IRAD asleep.

NOEMA.

WHY should I tell him more?   When last I raised
The veil behind which lies my sanctuary
Of inner life, he barely deigned to look,
But bade me share my superstitious realm
With Spirit consorts,—fit companions !
Why should this superciliousness wound,
When 'tis the low that at the lofty strikes,
Or they who soar be ruffled in their flight
By them who grovel ?   'Tis the feeble side
Of that in mortals which alone is strong,
To keep them feeble still : that sense of shame,
Which dreads to let the unfamiliar look

Upon our naked selves familiarly,
Even when noble in our nakedness.
Thus, when to Aran's misconceiving mind
I bare my heavenly secret, 'twere as though
I unto stranger gaze should bare myself,
And violate my instinct's modesty.
I cannot speak of it again to him !
Yet secrecy, like woodmite when it gnaws
A fruit upon the side that's next the tree,
Though marring not rotundity and bloom,
Eats out the heart withal.   Secretiveness
Is self's most subtle poison, and demands
The antidote of trust.   I'll trust my husband.
I hear him coming.

              [ARAN enters through a curtain in the tent.

           Must you go to-night ?

ARAN.

There is no must where a firm will presides,
And ordered Forethought, with its crown on top
And active sceptre in its hand, drives back
The rabble urgings of Necessity.
Must is a fiction of the Gods to fool
Their mortal serfs with ; a device for slaves,

Children, and women, and the sicklier sort.

But to the man whose mettle centuries

Of cowardly compliance have not quelled,

Must is a wrongful overt enemy,

Who must with overt rights be combated ;

Compelled to quit this usurped soil, and leave

A native field for resolution.

I go not to the Tower, because I must,

But, as my words have pushed it through the clouds,

Because I will.   Will shall be sovran here,

Will of the knitted front and tameless eyes,

While blind Necessity may reign in Heaven.

NOEMA.

Count it not sure, my lord, that Heaven is blind,

Or that this higher will which unto us,

Who cannot change it, seems necessity,

Is not deliberate option of the wise ;

Which to resist is but to coax defeat

To come and crush us.   Nay, mistrust your Tower,

Which, at its top, will fall as short of Heaven,

As all we win falls short of all we want.

Listen, one moment : Let me ask the Spirit,

That conversed with me, and whose pinions range

Over illimitable leagues of wind,
What distance may divide the Heavens from Earth,
And what long links man's energy must forge
To bring them into touch.

ARAN.

A Spirit, forsooth !
Ask of the kestrel how the stare should fly
To balk him when he swoops ; go ask the waves
How the scared bark should foil their turbulence ;
Or from the irate wrack and puckered clouds,
How best the thunder-threatened oak should wrap
His fluttering foliage round his agëd head,
To meet the lightning harmless !   When the wolf
No more shall raven through the scuttling flock,
But bear a crook and gently shepherd them ;
Then shall the aborigines of air
Cease to conspire against this solid Earth
And serve as Heaven's astute auxiliaries.
Could they affect to join their ranks to ours,
They were but traitors in the camp, and thou
Wert but a traitor too, wert not a dupe,
To harbour such a sly ambassador.

NOEMA.

O, but you wrong him!   He is frank as light,
Clear as the morning, candid as the noon,
And never impious subterfuge could lurk
In such transparent pinions.   He would do
All that I asked him, all that you might ask,
Would run my messages from stage to stage
Of the unsurveyed air, and bring you count
And exact measure of your enterprise.

ARAN.

A most obliging Spirit!   Use him then
If you can make him serviceable.   But,
It is a source suspect.   For from the hour
When the intrepid Lucifer was flung,
Since by misgiving Seraphim forsook,
Over Heaven's battlements, no Spirit, 'twould seem,
Hath dared to brew rebellion in the sky,
Or seek allies in man.   They live content
To serve celestial spleen and wreak us hurt ;
To be the messengers of poisons, plagues,
Blights, mildews, frosts, droughts, famines, hurricanes,
But never once have lent a fanning wing
To mortal aspiration.   Help from Spirits !

Why call them Spirits ?   Spirits spiritless !
When man's encouraging voice at length is heard
Resounding through the stars, and all abreast
We storm God's last intrenchments, then perchance
Will insurrection flame along the Spheres,
And their subservient denizens demand
To fight beneath our flag.   But, until then,
To hope for succour from their half-fledged wings,
Were as though one should look for tiger's teeth
Within the palate of the squealing hare ;
And Spirits' mission, spite their specious name,
Will be to harry men and hoodwink women.

NOEMA.

The Spirit that hath deigned to touch our home
Is of a gentle and considerate mould,
And would—nay, hear me !—prosper me and mine.
May I not therefore——

ARAN.

You may what you will,
So that you move no counsel 'gainst the Tower.
That would I never brook.

[Goes over to IRAD's crib and bends over.

                              Sleep sound, my boy,

Sleep sound and grow to manhood!   Would thou
     hadst
Already put on thy virility,
And couldst thy masculine ambition lend
To swell thy father's purpose!   I would wait,
But that my resolution might drop off
Whilst thine was ripening.   Thine the harvest be,
So that the seed and sickle fall to me.

                                        [Exit ARAN.

                    NOEMA (*alone*).

For male self-will there is no argument
That is not overborne.   He would not listen.
A man knows all before a woman speaks.
Who argues with his shadow?   It must follow,
Draw he which way he will.   Yet Spirits listen;
And mine submits to me as meek an ear
As though I were a Spirit, he but flesh.
Is it that spirit hearkens to the flesh
Easier than flesh to spirit?   That is a thought
Rips up the womb of darkness, and delivers
A ray of struggling light.   Yet I to him
Could hearken while the glass of time ran out

From day to night, then from night back again,
Nor ever think to fret the even stream
Of his discourse; and I am merest flesh.
It were presumptuous to hope otherwise.
So darkness sucks that glimmer back again,
And leaves us in obscurity.   Sleep, child !
Sleep, as he bade thee, soundly; nor awake
To learn how inharmonious is man's heart,
And how its discord grows with added strings.

SCENE II

Night.   The Moon.   AFRAEL standing on the edge of an
extinct volcano.

AFRAEL (*alone*).

Meseems as though this nighest stage to earth,
This uninhabited and jagged ball,
Were unto Earth a travelling tributary.
Betwixt yon living planet which is now
To my fixed passion chiefest point in space,
And this one, dead, whereon I·halt and bide
The hour to bid me sweep to my sweet tryst

The distance never widens nor yet wanes.
Yes, we are following, following, through the night,
Silently sailing in this azure sea,
Whose waves are all around, yet never whelm,
Along the track swayed by that pilot world.
Yet what a wreck this skyey bark appears !
Empty of spirits, empty of all life,
Pastureless, streamless, voiceless, tenantless ;
No sound, no movement ; silent as deep thought ;
Bare or of trunk or herb ; even no noise
Of falling waters or of flitting wing :
No growth and nought to grow in,—only bare rock,
Cavernous, rugged, huge, precipitous,
Rolled out in slippery unadvancing waves,
Volcanic writhings rigid now in death !
Is this the end of all fidelity
Unto the earthly ? Yet it follows still.
Perchance it is its fate to follow still,
Its punishment. Nay, rather let me think,
It is its supreme bliss, its one reward,
That thus outweighs all other penalties.
O melancholy wanderer ! I would be
Charred even as thou, extinguished, desolate,
With nought but rock and ashes at my core,

Sooner than once surrender that last right
Still to pursue and worship from afar.
Move on ! move on ! ye constellations calm,
That tell the watches of the night, and bring
Swiftly the hour I may indulge my love,
And leap the frontier of my banishment.
For æons unrecorded that mine eyes
Have watched yon marshalled vault, I ne'er have
     known ye
Hasten or slacken in your solemn march ;
But now to-night ye seem to me to lag,
And fall into the rear of Time, whose rhythm
Is marked but by mine own impatient heart.

SCENE III

The tents of ARAN. NOEMA, without, in the moonlight.

NOEMA.

If he came now I should be ta'en unarmed :
And, in this mystic hour of midmost night,
My heart would prove a traitor to my heart,
And help him seize its sleeping citadel.

He must not come ! he must not come to-night.
'Tis different in the gaze of barefaced day.
The earthy then is round us, clear and nigh,
And we are rudely minded of ourselves,
Our mundane substance, mortal accidents,
And the subservient company of ills
That wait upon our actions.   Then we see
In a too faithful mirror what we are,
And sadly doff night's fanciful array.
Then this repulsive gaoler, this coarse flesh,
Which on our aspirations keepeth ward,
Mockingly warns us not to dare too far
Beyond the precincts of our prison-house.
But dark confers a treacherous liberty,
And, veiling earthly semblance from the earth,
Gives unto things and shapes terrestrial
A heavenly complexion, even as now.
See, the cowled night seems rapt in mental prayer
Before the dim shrine of eternity.
There moveth nothing mortal in the air,
Nor on the ground ; but, in the dewy grass
And spangled vault, absolute ecstasy.
It is the hour when, finding reason foiled,
Love presses home his final argument,

And touches his conclusion.   O sweet Night !

Thou art the very atmosphere of love,

And every star proclaims thee amorous.

'Twere too much for a mortal, came he now.

Detain him in the sky, ye twinkling orbs,

That must have power to charm, lest that I should

Be in his bright propinquity consumed.

But hark !   What sings ?   There is no other voice

Of such unclouded music.   It is he !

And Fate hath had no pity on my fears.

                    [AFRAEL descends, singing.

It was in music that he took farewell,

In music he returns.   But when he showed

On the blue background of the shining morn,

His outline shone but as a ridge of cloud,

Flecked by a rising but still hidden moon.

Now burns he brighter than the brightest star,

And makes illumination in the air.

Oh ! he is beautiful beyond the range

Even of clear imagination's eye,

And Fancy, in creative madness, ne'er

Projected such a vision !

SCENE IV

AFRAEL.

Hail! beloved!

NOEMA.

Hail! gracious Spirit!   But I pray thee, come
No nearer than thou art, but deign allow
For the infirmity of mortal gaze.
My sight is almost blinded even now,
And nearer brightness would but leave me dark.

AFRAEL.

Fear not!   Thou must my nature closer prove,
And with my aspect grow familiar.
They will not hurt thee.   Spirit cannot hurt,
Though it at first may dazzle.   Oh! I thought
The hours would never pass, and that the night,
Climbing the upward steep of dark had paused,
And lost herself in sudden drowsiness.
Now on the very topmost point she stands,
Surveying mute her wide dominions,
And I, attentive to the time, am here.

NOEMA.

Yes, thou art punctual as the sun himself.
But love was ne'er a laggard.

AFRAEL.

Tell me then,
Now with those eyes that seem the lamps of truth,
And with those lips that are its oracle,
Thou lovest me!

NOEMA.

How may I, mortal, love
Thee, an immortal Spirit?   Yet if to yearn
To dwell in the soft shadow of thy wings,
To live in the strange music of thy voice,
And to be bathed in the celestial light
Thy presence radiates, indication be
Of the heart's fever, how shall I deny
I love thee?   'Tis the Spirit that I love,
Though Spirit have I none to love thee with.
Look!   I love that to which I may not soar;
Thou lovest that to which thou canst not stoop.
Could mortal with immortal ever blend,

I need had answered otherwise.   But all
Is contradiction here, and reason gives
No hint to instinct in perplexity.

AFRAEL.

So that thou lovest me, I care not how ;
Nor should we let straightforward feeling lose
Itself in tortuous reason's labyrinth.
Come, let us for the empyrean start,
Now, now while still the rarely-buoyant breath
Of that avowal will inflate our flight,
And the moon lends her lamp to point the track.

NOEMA.

This is the sheer insanity of love,
To think, because 'twere sweet to do it, thou canst
Lift me, thus deeply anchored in the flesh,
And bear me through that unresisting sea
Where only unsubstantial Spirits sail.

AFRAEL.

Then see the power of love's insanity !
Lo ! from this petty port of earth we break,
And through the shoreless ocean of the air,

Where continent is none, and starry isles
Are all that dot its blue immensity,
Sailless we sail!

NOEMA.

Oh! we have quit the ground,
And stand on air!   I own thy wondrous power;
But be content with its brief exercise,
And render me to earth while yet 'tis time.

AFRAEL.

O my most lightsome burden! what dost fear?
Dost thou not feel, even as I, that 'tis
The even wings of love that bear us on?
See! not a plume of my own pinion moves,
But in its downy crevices thy head,
Thy golden-tressëd head, recumbent rests.
Dread nothing, thou fair load!   I feel thy weight
No more than thou dost mine.

NOEMA.

How fast, how fast
The earth recedes from us!   I just can see
The glittering roofs of home which dearer grow

As grow they dimmer, and the convex tops
Of the tall palm-trees gleam like drops of dew,
Drinking the moonlight.   Now I nought descry
But the bold stem of the defiant Tower,
Which seems to follow.   What, if Irad woke !
My beautiful Irad ! if he came to harm !
When, when shall we return ?

AFRAEL.

Almost as soon
As the moon takes to clear herself from cloud,
When first she rises in a dappled sky,
Contending with obstruction.

NOEMA.

Now, we seem
To be upon a level with her light,
And like as though she raced us through the air.
How large and luminous she seems !

AFRAEL.

We are
As far from Earth as she is, and from her
But half such journey.   Even as we speak,
Behold ! she drops below us.

NOEMA.

Ay, and seems
From us to move as whilom did the Earth,
Though we appear self-poised and motionless.

AFRAEL.

'Tis an illusion of thy earthly sense,
Thou canst not all subdue. She moves, but we
Move yet more quickly.

NOEMA.

Smaller now she wanes,
Shining no larger than when seen from Earth.
And look! there is a planet under us,
Twinkling like Saturn, and about as far
Beneath, as he above on winter nights.
What may it be?

AFRAEL.

That is the Earth, we have left.

NOEMA.

The Earth! It is as bright as any star.

H

AFRAEL.

Because it is a star, and all the stars   ·
Have this much earthly in their government,
They are the mirrors, not the face of light ;
Reflecting the great aspect of the sun,
Which, in himself too bright to look upon,
Would else through trackless space shine on unglassed.

NOEMA.

But is Earth hung in space ?

AFRAEL.

                    Through space it moves,
Since that in space is nothing stationary.
For motion, mastering all things, sets them free,
That else would rot in sluggish servitude.

NOEMA.

Do stars in aught beside resemble Earth ?

AFRAEL.

There is no star like to another star ;
Nor doth the faintest-twinkling asteroid

Find anywhere its twin.   Infinite change
Through infinite succession sways the air.

NOEMA.

And hast thou seen them all?

AFRAEL.

                              Seen all the stars?
No! nor shall ever see them.   Some there be
That I have followed, followed, followed still,
And still, still followed, till my wings waxed faint,
But never overtook.   Others there are,
Toward which I have strained my flight for days, for
        nights,
And days again succeeding, faster far
Than we have journeyed hither, and their light
Ne'er grew one glimmer brighter to my gaze,
Their radius one span broader.   Nor do I doubt
That beyond these, yet other planets glow,
Whose distance unattainable compared
With other, farther constellations still,
Is nearness' self.   Why, look around thee now!
Skies that were late thy canopy, are spread
A glittering carpet far beneath thy feet;

And stars which gleamed like crowns beyond thy
 reach,
Now like a jewelled girdle hem thee round.
Yet, some bright orbs thou still must recognise,
Nightly familiar to thine earthly ken,
Which are as deeply buried in the blue
High overhanging firmament, as when
We lightly bounded from that carnal ball,
We now can see no more.

NOEMA.

     How wonderful!
But I begin to faint in this thin air,
And to my dim disordered gaze the stars
Grow giddy, and the constellations swim.
The planets circle wildly, and the sky
Pales to a misty shroud, which, closing in
With ever-dwindling hollow, stifles me.
Ah! I can fetch no breath!

AFRAEL.

     Then let me draw
Thy fair face upward, till thy shining hair
Falls over thee and me, indifferently,

And, on this shoulder rested, thy warm cheek
Finds a forgetful pillow, where thou mayst
Live by my lips and feed thy breath with mine !
There ! Dost not breathe anew ?

NOEMA.

O yes ! with breath
Freer and fuller than I e'er have drawn,
And infinitely sweeter ! Lo ! the stars
Resume their stern serenity and keep
Their high appointed places, and the sky
Once more recedes, and blue, blue grows the vault,
And clear the vision of eternal space.

AFRAEL.

And art thou happy ? Tell me thou art happy.

NOEMA.

It is no mortal rapture that I feel,
But a strange undercurrent of delight,
Which flows I know not whitherward.   But hark !
Surely I heard ethereal music dying
On the attendant air ?

AFRAEL.

                    Thou hast an ear
Quickly attuned to heavenly cadences.
Yes, they are singing in yon nearest stars,
We flit past now.

NOEMA.

          May we not halt and listen ?

AFRAEL.

Listen, then.   They sing.

FIRST STAR.

I am the star of the Mystic Number,
    Breathing the sacred sign
On the brow and the breast of them that slumber,
    Drowsed in a dream divine;
But when they awake, I their soul forsake,
    And my spell remaineth mine.

SECOND STAR.

I am the star of the Past and Future,
    I am Eternity's star,

And the weft and the woof without seam or suture
Of Time I cross and bar,
Endlessly spinning the Never-Beginning,
And linking the Near and Far. '

THIRD STAR.

I am the Star of the Unforbidden,
I am the Absolute Star,
And, since Ever, with gleaming crest have ridden
Afront the unswerving car,
That noiselessly rolls unto unguessed goals
Upon winds that were and are.

NOEMA.

What strange seraphic melodies ! albeit
Through the dull cover of my fleshly sense
The tenuous drift of spiritual song
Scarce penetrates.

AFRAEL.

Nor wholly even to me.
For music is not meant to speak like speech,
But, like to gleams of sunshine now we see,
Now lose, discerned is but at intervals ;

Whose silences withal by finer ears
Are clearly apprehended.   Music is
An under-aspect of the Universe,
A faint expression, quickly ebbed away
Into itself, beyond life's boundaries.

NOEMA.

Doth every constellation chant like these?

AFRAEL.

Not all the stars alone, but all things sing.
The smallest mote that flickers in the sun,
Still as it shines keeps humming to itself,
Lending no less than the high-quiring Spheres
Distinctive but agreeing voice to aid
The universal concert.   Not the winds,
These shrilly-throated choristers whose strain
Floats on the deep-toned cloudland's thunder-fugues,
Not the aggressive waves that roar and rise
Above the feeble trebles of the air,
Though they be heard more plainly, swell the choir,
Ruled by the unseen wand of Nature, more
Than Time harmonic, than melodious Space,
Rhythmical numbers, shapes symphonious,

Darkness, and distance, light, proximity,
An endless diapason.   All is song.
And if the music of one part could cease,
The whole would perish with it, and were then
One silent undistinguishable void.
But say, art happy still, here in these heights,
Thou late didst pusillanimously deem
Even by love were inaccessible?

NOEMA.

Happy?   That word too weighted is with flesh
To speak the floating exultation felt
In this rare region; and my fancy dreams
I feel what thou must feel when steering smooth,
Alone, in these thy native latitudes;
That, as I soar, I liker grow to thee,
Till, all unconscious of the cumbrous load
Which is my very consciousness below,
I seem to be of carnal rind disrobed,
And not so much a tenant of the sky
As a mere skyey shape or fantasy,
Shifting with every current of the air,
And owing all sensation unto it.
Say do I limn thy life, and dost thou feel

Like this, when thine imponderable form,
By me unhampered, buoyantly ascends
Unto those heights, to which these heights are depths?

AFRAEL.

Thou hast described it rarely, but not told
How the affections of thy frame are stirred
Towards him who brought thee hither.   Lovest me
　　more,
Or lovest me less, now that we sail serene
Through unconditioned ether, and respire
The breath that feeds the brightly-throbbing stars?

NOEMA.

More, measurelessly more ! for there below
I did not, dared not, love thee.   I was cramped
By the chill shackles of forbidding fear,
By the injunctions of distrustful sense,
And much which thou, a Spirit, wot'st not of.
Here am I free to let my longings range
Up all the heights of Spiritual space,
Where, as it seems to my unfettered pulse,
There only rule the Infinite and thou,
Which are as one, whom I, their subject, serve.

But thou, thou dost not tell me of thy love,
As when we clung to Earth.   Is it that here,
Here in this rarefied and subtle realm,
While love of mortal for immortal burns
To a befitting spire of purity,
That of immortal for a mortal finds   `
No proper medium, and hence all goes out?

AFRAEL.

Not all.   Nor could the very topmost top
Of heavenliest Heaven that flame so rarefy,
That it should issue in a vaporous void.
Yet, will I own, that strange volcanic want,
Which hotly in the nether world convulsed
My being, still kept subsiding as we soared,
Till, in this final zenith of our quest,
My love is more like memory than hope,
Like stalled content than roaming appetite.

NOEMA.

Alas! I fear that thou dost love me less
Than once thou didst.   Then let us back to Earth!

AFRAEL.

Swift, an thou wilt.   But when we reach the Earth,
Wilt thou once more lock up this heaving breast,
Fearlessly bared under the firmament?

NOEMA.

Earth will demand its forfeit doubtlessly
For such a daring trespass, since the skies
Seem to begrudge us perfect happiness.
Thou from the sapphire element must swoop
And taste the gray dull atmosphere of Earth,
Ere through thy wings the thrill of mortal love
Can make itself a channel; whilst that I
Need to be lifted to inhuman heights,
Before the vile integument falls off
Which there betrays my lowly lineage,
And I surrender my essential self
To lofty sympathies.   O Fate perverse !
Thus never are we balanced, but the scales
Of Spirit and sense alternate sink and rise,
And one but helps the other out of reach.

AFRAEL.

Is there no even region of the air

In which Love's dual bliss may trembling hang,
Yet never lose its equilibrium?
Lo! comes the moon, the furrowed moon, in sight,
And as we near Earth's careworn tributary,
Again the strange tumultuous trouble seems
To ripple through my pinions, and I grow
More intimately conscious thou art there,
There with each warmly undulating tress,
There with thy temples smooth, there with thine eyes,
Thy faintly parted lips, thy dimpled throat,
And all thy solid shapely attributes.

NOEMA.

Speak me not thus! for I begin to grow
Too much aware of my gross quality,
To own this lumpish body, and thy words
But hammer deeper in my ringing brain
That penetrating knowledge.

AFRAEL

Shall we then
Ascend once more toward the cerulean dome,
Beneath whose never-reached but nearer vault
This misty trouble of the flesh would seem

To be dispelled? Say yes but with thine eyes,
And up we soar, swifter than now we sink,
Into the lap of unimagined zones,
There to be lulled in vague beatitude.
Say quickly, quickly! for behold! the moon
No longer is below us, and the sheen
Of her straight light strikes on thy pallid face.

NOEMA.

No! hasten we adown! and never again
Must I, poor earthly mendicant, invade
The rich celestial palace of the sky.
Tell me, O tell me, we are descending still.

AFRAEL.

Swift as a Spirit ever can descend.
See, sails the moon above us now, and look!
We dip into a silvery cloud, which speaks
That we have crossed the frontier that divides
The hazeless Heavens from Earth's outlying mist.

NOEMA.

Then let us part at this clear boundary
Betwixt our hostile homes; thee to thy sky,

Thy happy sky, me to sad Earth repair.

Thou that hast had the witchery to uplift

This sordid burden to resplendent spheres,

Enough of heavenly cunning sure dost own

To drop me gently down, through what remains

Of intervening void, to dullard Earth,

While thou, delivered from this carnal clod,

Wingest thy way in joyful solitude

Through undetermined spaces, me forgot

Amid the rapturous singing of the stars.

But now I know that we are nearing Earth :

I feel so heavy, and so like to sink.

AFRAEL.

My lightness lighter grows as we descend,

And through the denser volume of the air

I drop with effort.

NOEMA.

Ah ! there blabs the truth !

I help to drag thee down.

AFRAEL.

There, is the Tower

Splitting the night.

NOEMA.

Then, are we very near.
How impotent and feeble now it seems!
Why, were the Earth piled all on end, it would
Scarce make a visible finger-post to Heaven.
And there! I see the snow-white tents of home
Smooth in the moonlight, and the palm-trees tall,
Those never-changing sentinels, that stand
Mute at the portals.   Heed lest we alight
On their broad tops. . . . I dizzy grow once more,
And—and——

SCENE V

The Earth.   The tents of ARAN.

AFRAEL.

Behold! in safety you alight.

[NOEMA enters the chief tent, and hurries to the spot
where she left IRAD sleeping.

NOEMA.

My boy! my boy!   Art safe within thy crib,
Or have the dark divinities of air

Pilfered my earthly treasure, to amerce

My unpermitted trespass on their fields ?

No ! there he lies, all coiled into himself,

A heap of rosy sleep ; one chubby hand

Dimpling the pillow, while his unkempt curls

Over the delicate sinless temples stray,

And a warm moisture dews his round, soft cheeks.

Oh ! thou art fairer to thy mother's eye

Than brightest constellation, and her choice

Would be to sit enslaved to thy small wants,

Rather than sweep the skies from end to end

Upon the pinions of sublime desire !

[She snatches him up, and kisses him tenderly.

IRAD (*waking*).

What is it, mother?

NOEMA.

Nothing, my sweet boy,

Save that I love thee, and desire to fold

Thy form within my arms.   Now, sleep again,

And the light wings of unseen angels be

Thy curtain, and their hymns thy lullaby !

[Exit from the tent, and returns to the open air.

I

AFRAEL.

You found him, as you left him, fast asleep :
We have been gone so shortly.

NOEMA.

Yes, he slept.

AFRAEL.

His name I know, for I have heard thee say it,
But even now am ignorant of thine.

NOEMA.

They call me Noema.

AFRAEL.

What a sweet name !
Liquid as dew.

NOEMA.

Are Spirits signified
By sounding appellations, like ourselves ?

AFRAEL.

I in my star as Afrael am known.

NOEMA.

Then to thy star, O Afrael, return,
For we must part!

AFRAEL.

And when to meet again?

NOEMA.

When Heaven and Earth shall meet, but not before.

AFRAEL.

They have met now, for they have met in thee.

NOEMA.

Only because thy fantasy projects
Thyself in me, no otherwise.

AFRAEL.

Noema!
I feel a want I never felt before,—
A want to be like you! to own your form,
Your flesh, your strange, resisting properties.
For now I cannot touch you as I would;
And as I strain to fold my wings around

Your body beautiful, I fail to clutch
Its definite perfections, and they seem
Still to escape, while my own being thrills
With purposeless strong motions, like a wind
That blows, and blows, with nought to blow against.

NOEMA.

O, you have caught contagion from the flesh ;
And I can only bid you swift return
Up to yon pure and passionless domicile,
And leave this squalid tenement, this me,
To its degraded inmates, whose defect
It is to grovel on their native ground,
Nor feed on aught beyond.

AFRAEL.

Have you forgot so soon what lofty joy
Your lightened senses took in the upper world ?
But I will talk no more to you of Earth,
Nor of the new affections it hath bred
Within my bosom, but my constant speech,
Like to myself, shall to the skies revert,
So you again be my companion.

Come with me now, or come when next you will,
But yield me this assurance, that henceforth
My heavenly tent of blue, no winds uproot,
Shall be your residence, or that at least
You there will choose your home, and make below
But rare and hasty sojourn, borne by me
Backward and forward, but with me alway.

NOEMA.

How fatuous is love! Deem you that I,
That I, poor worm, for ever could discard
This crawling coat and prone defect of flesh,
And, fledged with lightness, flit from star to star,
Or, an I might, that their invaded fires
Would not resent my wings, and I should drop,
A shrivelled nauseous cinder, back to Earth?
Already like a dream the memory floats
Of that outrageous journey, and I shudder,
Thinking of such a venture safe surpassed.

AFRAEL.

Make it once more with me, then will you know
It is no dream, and nought to shudder at.

NOEMA.

O no! no! no!   In gardens of the air
I an exotic were, and quick should pine
For the moist soil of Earth!   You cannot guess
Maternity's sweet servitude, nor know
How tightly mothers hug their self-wrought chains.
Amid the splendid vastness of the skies,
Charmed by your voice, charmed by the planets'
    song,
And my dwarf nature magnified by yours,
My ears would listen for my Irad's shout,
My lips grow drouthy for his April kiss,
And all my heart feel empty, because drained
Of the sweet freshening waters which he struck
Straight from this arid desert rock, when first
I felt him struggling feebly in my womb.
Leave me! nay, leave me! and return to Heaven!

AFRAEL.

Return to Heaven!   That were impossible,
Save you come too!   You have unheavened the
    Heavens.
But do you, then, love Irad;—him alone?

NOEMA.

I said not so.

AFRAEL.

But—but—you love him more
Than—all; than anything?

NOEMA.

Nay, press me not!
Enough! I could not leave him.

AFRAEL.

Let him come.
You him shall bear, and I will bear you both.
For he would love to ride upon the air,
Gambol among the soft unhurtful clouds,
And make his playmates of the wandering winds,
As childish and unpurposed as himself.
Why do you hesitate?

NOEMA.

I do not hesitate: I am resolved.

AFRAEL.

Resolved to banish me! to make my wings
But exiles in their native territory,
And, in the very air where I was fledged,
Doom me to roam a stranger!

NOEMA.

       Even so,
If so it even must be. Now, farewell!
The Night begins to waver in her sleep,
And dream uneasily; she soon will wake.
Did you not hear a shiver in the trees?

AFRAEL.

Drive me away not yet!

NOEMA.

      I must! I must!
The parley at the Tower must now be closed,
And Aran even now be on his way.

AFRAEL.

May I not linger till he comes?

NOEMA.

No! no!
For that were—— But indeed you must not stay!
I see a something moving through the gloom.
It will be he. Did you not hear a step?

AFRAEL.

Nor hear nor see I aught, but you alone.
When first I was your guest, you bade me bide
Till Aran's coming.

NOEMA.

'Twas different then. . . . Go! As you love me, go!

AFRAEL.

Then go I must. But when may I return?

NOEMA.

Not soon; no, nor for long: I fain would say,
Never! but cannot say it! Go, go now!
I hear his footstep: I am sure 'tis he!
I must go in, and leave you.

AFRAEL.

Then, farewell!

[He folds his wings widely around her.

Farewell, but not for ever!

[He unfolds his wings, ascends into the air, gazing back,
but silent, and disappears.

NOEMA.

Gone!   He is gone!

And I it was that sent him!   O, come back!

Come back, and fold me in thy plumes once more,

And kiss me, not at one particular point,

But, as it seemed, with all thy wings at once!

'Tis well he cannot hear me.   Maybe, he doth.

I will go in.   How giddy I do feel!

Those wings!   Those wings! . . . This is the way, I
think,

And this . . . what an embrace! . . . this, this the
spot

Where Irad—Irad. . . . Come to me, my boy!

[She swoons against the crib where IRAD soundly sleeps.

SCENE VI

NOEMA still lying senseless against IRAD'S crib.   IRAD asleep.
Enter ARAN.

ARAN (*rousing* NOEMA).

What ails thee, Noema?   Why liest thou here?
Why not abed and sleeping?

NOEMA (*slowly opening her eyes*).

Afrael! . . .

Ha! Aran!

ARAN.

Yes : whom else wouldst thou expect?

NOEMA.

None, surely.   But I was not yet awake.
I must have fallen asleep.

[Rises from the ground.

What can I get thee?

ARAN.

Nothing.

NOEMA.

What happened at the Tower to-night?

ARAN.

I baffled them still better than this morn.
And, ere another week of bondage crawls
To its tame end, will our determined point
Confront the haughty firmament, eye to eye,
And with Earth's menace equal Heaven's disdain.
Yet Peleg plots to balk me still, and finds
In Korah an accomplice. Dreamers both,
And slaves to the Unseen! 'Tis action wins,
And common wants, led by uncommon will.

NOEMA.

Betwixt the seen and the Unseen who shall draw
Infallible distinction? Couldst behold
What I this night beheld, thou wouldst no more
Tether thy reason to some narrow plot,
But give it scope to range through fenceless space,
With Fancy for its consort.

ARAN.

What didst thou see?

NOEMA.

I saw the Heavens and all the world of air,
And festive Midnight's burnished cressets swung,
Invisibly, and in their motion free,
From the deep azure ceiling of the sky.
And I heard the planets sing, and watched the Earth
Dwindle in distance to a doubtful speck,
Then dwarfed beyond the cunning of the eye
To say 'twas anywhere.

ARAN.

                    I doubt thee not,
For thou wert ever of a dreaming mind,
Nor, when I caught thee prone by Irad's crib,
That thou such flimsy visions didst conceive.
But what of that?   Sure now thou art awake,
And seest the Unseen was not seen at all.
How wouldst thou help our unfantastic work?
For somnolency's fumes yet never baked
One solid brick, nor slumber's filmy stuff
Provide the stable slime to set it with.

NOEMA.

'Twas in no dream that I the Heavens beheld,

But with the open eyes that on thee look.
Whilst thou didst hold convention at the Tower,
I through ethereal regions piercing soared,
And proved, with my own sense, that did each
    course
Of thy presumptuous masonry annul
A league, and not a span, thou still wouldst strain
More idly at the sky than Irad doth,
A-tiptoe, toward some tantalising toy,
By thee at arm's-length held above thy head.

ARAN.

Spread thyself now one foot above the ground,
And stay there twenty seconds !

NOEMA.

            Oh ! I could not.
Earth lets not earth unaided quit its side ;
'Tis too exacting.   Spirit it was that loosed
My inert matter from the ground, and bore
This burden upward ; the same comely Spirit,
Who came unto our tents one twilight eve,
And twice hath come again.

ARAN.

And ever comes,
When there is none but thou to testify.
Conclusive witness ! . . . Why, if Irad, there,
Babbled such folly, thou wouldst purge him straight,
Or whip him into soundness.   Get thee to bed,
And sleep thyself—back into sanity !

[Exit.

NOEMA.

Back into sanity !   Am I insane ?
Sometimes it well would seem so.   For the hold
Which this conjunction with the gross maintains
Upon my lighter essence, bids me doubt
The wisdom of my longings to escape.
Yes, it *is* madness, to aspire beyond
The unyielding limits of our quality ;
And sanity, which turns the homely spit,
Trudges its narrow round contentedly,
And sups with satisfaction.   Sane I am not,
Or life's recurring service would suffice.
Were it not well to touch the rest in all,
Touching them in so much ?   I have a body,
Sight, hearing, sense, members, and appetites,

Needs, aches, fatigues, pleasures, infirmities,

Twin unto theirs.   Why then not twin all round?

Because I am insane, and they are not.

Is that the reason?   Did I only dream

That I surveyed the Heavens?   O no! no!

For dreams may be recalled, but never yet

Were dreams felt after waking; and I feel

The tingling sense of those enfolding wings

Even more than when they closely wrapped me
        round,

And shook me to convulsive consciousness.

O sweet insanity! take all that's sane,

And leave me nought but madness!

> [She again sinks into a swoon.

END OF ACT III

ACT IV

SCENE I

The upper air.   Deep night.   AFRAEL alone.

AFRAEL.

" Not soon, no, nor for long ! " How soon ? How long ?
All soon is late, all long vain longing seems,
Since last I looked on her. . . . " I fain would say,
Never ! but cannot say it." Yet it feels
Even now as though that Never were my doom.
And she by Love enjoined me ! O safe chain !
Which he who wears is plighted not to break,
Thou art as light and frail as gossamer,
Yet Fate could forge none tighter. When will it
    end,
This temporary banishment that seems
More than eternal ? I have lingered oft
Around her dwelling when she was not there,

And, hovering o'er her tent whenas she slept,
Returned to ether, empty!

[He soars silently higher into the air and poises again.

What an expanse!
Worlds upon worlds, and stars on stars revolve,
Through still-beginning distance. Systems vast
Within yet outer systems spacious move,
And these but inner to yet other rounds,
Themselves but puny circles shut in space.
Yet care I for one only merest mote
Within this shining concave unconvexed,
One speck whereof I ne'er surrender sight,
But still keep plying a short restless wing,
From this last point whence gleams it visible,
To where it round dilates and fills the eye;
Then again back, thence back again once more,
In ceaseless iteration! Other track
Know I not now, nor have I any flight
For all the countless avenues of Heaven.

[He descends rapidly once more, nor pauses till he
reaches the Earth, where he alights on the topmost
storey of the Tower.

What a high perch! This is a wondrous work,
And wondrous they who build it, even if vain.

How big and black it leans against the night,

Sleeping on darkness ! 'Tis a giddy height,

Even for one who gazes from the sky

Into the deeps of space ; for, there, no top,

Nor bottom, nor between, resists the sense,

And all is absolute ; but here the eye,

Shrinking to what it looks on, makes compare,

And finds an awful contrast.   How deserted,

Silent, and still !   No figure flits or moves

On its prodigious balconies ; no step

Stirs on the spiral rounds of its huge stairs,

And, coiled within its walls, even Echo sleeps.

Why cannot Spirits sleep ?   O would that I

Could ever and anon in slumber sheathe

This too sharp edge of wakeful appetite,

That cuts the sense so keenly ! . . . What was that ?

Methought I heard the waving of a wing,

And even felt its sweep.   No ! it was nought.

No Spirits hie this way.   I see the stars,

But from their occupants have strayed remote.

I stand above the things that nightly sleep.

Lo ! yonder is her tent !   *She* sleeps within,

And I watch here, no nearer than if hosts

Of roomy constellations rolled between.

She doth not even know that I am here;
Yet her inert unconsciousness hath power
To draw and keep me towards her.

A VOICE.

Afrael!

AFRAEL.

Who calls my name? What wouldst thou have with
me?

SECOND VOICE.

What wouldst *thou* have? Thou art a Spirit by birth,
By Spirit still unfed.

AFRAEL.

Who question me?
I hear you speak, but cannot fix your forms.

THIRD VOICE.

We are but Voices; Voices are not seen.
Answer, if thou wouldst find a remedy
To the defect thou wailest thus aloud.

AFRAEL.

I am enamoured of a mortal shape.

FIRST VOICE.

We know it, or we had not questioned thee.
But what with mortal shape hast thou to do?
What wantest thou with her?

AFRAEL.

                                With her to dwell:
In the high Heavens, or on the lowlier Earth,
But somewhere, anywhere, so not apart
From her who draws me ever!

SECOND VOICE.

                                Knowest thou not,
She in the Heavens, a mortal, cannot dwell,
Though with audacious pinions thou hast once
That child of dust obtruded on the sky?
She is on Earth: on Earth she must abide.

AFRAEL.

Then let me thither drop, to abide there too!
The Heavens have lost their savour, and the light
Of the interminable ether seems
But darkness more apparent. She is my sun;
And all is tenebrous where she is not.

THIRD VOICE.

Saner than thou, she knoweth that no Spirit
Can be her consort; that a ban as dim,
But indestructible, as that which holds
Darkness and light, silence and sound, apart,
Keeps thee and her asunder.   Ye cannot blend,
While thou immortal, mortal she, remains.

AFRAEL.

Then let me doff this immortality,
Which is but immortality of want,
And be a mortal, wanting only her,
But crowning want with winning!

FIRST VOICE.

                    Thou art aware,
For she herself hath told thee, what it is
To be a mortal.   Thou wouldst surely die.

AFRAEL.

Better to live and die, than not to live:
And this is vacancy; this is not life.

SECOND VOICE.

Bethink thee yet again !

AFRAEL.

Oh ! I have thought
Till thinking is a weariness. If ye
Have power to clip these useless wings, and fix
My limber essence to some mortal type,
Exert it now !

THIRD VOICE.

We have no power ; for we
Are Voices only. Force resides elsewhere,
Where thou must seek it.

AFRAEL.

Where ? Quick, tell me where !

FIRST VOICE.

The force thou seekest for, is lodged on Earth.
There only wilt thou find it.

AFRAEL.

I have been there,
But thence returned with only a vague want,

A penetrating hunger, a desire
That droops for lack of kindred nourishment,
That droops but dies not.

SECOND VOICE.

Ask thy mortal love.
She can assist thee.

AFRAEL.

How?

THIRD VOICE.

By mortal Love!
She can endue thee with consuming flesh,
And burn thy wings to ashes.   Tell her that,
And see if she will aid thee.

AFRAEL.

What!   If she
But once consent to help me rend the film
Which floats between us, I shall then assume
A mortal semblance, and, with flesh equipped,
Be armed to live, her life's companion?

FIRST VOICE.

So !

SECOND VOICE.

Even so !

THIRD VOICE.

Ay, even so it is !

AFRAEL.

And when may I demand this certain boon ?

[A pause.

The Voices answer not.   Are ye then gone,
Ye misty messengers ?   Speak once again,
If to assure me that I heard aright ;
That ye were Voices verily, and not
Mere echoes of soliloquising love.
Where hide ye, unseen promptings ?

A VOICE.

Afrael !

AFRAEL.

O what a melancholy Voice was that !
Distinct from any of the trinity

That hailed me first.   Sad Voice! why dost thou call,
Or why at least respond not?

ANOTHER VOICE.

                    Afrael!

AFRAEL.

Another wailing tongue!   What ails the air,
That it is charged with sadness, and my name
Seems the one sigh that lifts its weariness?
O that the curtain of the night would split,
And show the morning!   For I then should fly,
To her who hath no torments in her tongue,
From these distressful weepings of the wind.

VOICES.

Afrael! Afrael! wilt thou leave us, Afrael?

AFRAEL.

Be still, ye droning sycophants of woe!
Ye servile specious mourners! or float up
To yonder ether fanciful, that is
Like to yourselves, pale and impalpable.
Thus do I quit you!

                    [He lifts his wings, and leaving the Tower,
                        wends his way through the air.

SCENE II

The hour before dawn. The sky dark and troubled. Rising
ground on the outskirts of a wood. An altar of fagots, on
which lies a white he-goat, its feet bound, and its horns
wreathed with flowers. PELEG—KORAH—a crowd of
Bondmen.

PELEG.

Wait till the first streaks of the crimson dawn,

The unspeaking heralds of the Lord, announce

He with His hand hath driven away the dark,

And given the daylight leave to move from sleep.

He made the sea, He made the solid land,

Stars, and the moon, and the unquenchëd light

Of the round-rolling sun.   He made them all.

He raised His arm, and lo ! the mountains swelled,

Obedient to His drawing.   He breathed, and straight

The waters fled before Him, and the torrents,

Following the channels of His glancing eye,

Took their allotted courses.   The deep sea

He scooped out with the hollow of His hand,

And spake, and swift the great waves filled it up,

And took their moaning from His mighty voice.

The thunders are His messengers, the clouds
His footstool, and the winds fulfil His word.
Fear then the Lord your God, for He is great,
Encompassing the things He made, and sworn
To be avenged on them that fear Him not.

[He pauses and gazes at the eastern sky.

The dawn yet breaks not, for the Lord your God
Is angry with His people.   Ye have strayed
Far from His paths, have hearkened not His voice,
And now the earth's foundations are disturbed,
And tremble at His wrath.   The tempests wake,
And are grown livid with your wickedness.
Ye have forsaken His commands, and ta'en
The ordinance of man upon your backs,
And builded up yon proud rebellious Tower,
To pry into His secrets, that He hides
Within the dazzling darkness of the Heavens.
I will beseech His mercy, that He stay
The scourge of His right hand, and seek to turn
The straightness of His anger with the smoke
And savour of this whole-burnt-offering.
For He doth love the flesh of kids and goats,
When tendered Him with pure and humble hearts.

But tarries still the dawn, and ye must bide
The lifting of His eyelids.

> [He turns away to the altar, and the Bondmen gather
> round, KORAH and SIDON in their midst.

CROWD OF BONDMEN.

Korah speaks.

Let us hear Korah ; Korah ever leans
Upon the bondman's side.

KORAH.

Yes, friends ! I lean
Toward the feeble and oppressed ; and ye
Are crushed like corn, ay, beaten with the flail
Of the oppressor's greed.   If ye avert
Your eyes from Heaven, now whither shall ye turn ?
The ground is set against you, and the lords
Of the abundant earth begrudge your mouths
The forage for your limbs, and grind you down,
Even as the corn is ground between the stones,
And the stones eat not.   Look ! I bid ye take
Earth, and Earth's fulness, and the fruits thereof,
Nor from its harvests wish to be estranged.
Ye are Earth's sons, like as your tyrants are,
And, like your tyrants, ye must wring the soil

Till it gives forth its treasures.   But while Heaven

Stands on your side, with Heaven remain allied,

And listen unto Peleg when he prays.

Hark ! he would speak to you again.

> [PELEG turns again to the people. As he does
> so, the first red streaks of dawn appear in
> the sky, and a crowd of Freemen are seen
> hurrying up, led by ARAN.

PELEG.

Now doth the Lord command His unseen hosts

To strike the tents of darkness, and up-furl

The skirts of night and slumber ; and the day

Comes forth apparelled from His glorious hand.

So will we offer now a holocaust,

This ram without a stain, and cry to Him,

To spare His people, even though they have,

Urged by the wicked, planted yon tall Tower

Full in His presence !

> [The crowd of Bondmen begin to be agitated, to
> whisper among themselves, and to turn their
> eyes in the direction of the rapidly approach-
> ing Freemen. PELEG continues.

Hitherward they come,

The wicked who have urged you.   But, stand firm,

And put your trust in Him in Whose just sight

Bondmen are free, freemen are slaves, so these
Rebel against His face, and those obey.

KORAH.

Yes, flinch not, worthy friends ! Now is the hour
To rise against your chains and shake them off.
Tower or no Tower, why should ye hew them wood
And draw them water ? They have arms like you.
Are ye not flesh and blood ? What more are they,
That they should wield the whip, and ye should wince
Beneath its whistling swoop ?

[The Freemen rush up, with ARAN at their head.

ARAN.

How now, ye slaves !
What mean your truant faces, and from whom
Gat ye this empty-handed leave to-day ?
'Tis not the seventh morn, and if it were,
Ye shall not loose your palms without our nod.
A pretty tale ! whilst flag the kilns for breath,
And the raw slime in unmixed puddles lies,
To turn your slothful backs upon the Tower,
And pipe and frisk beside a summer wood !

Back to your work, or we will flog you to't!
Who hath begot this mutiny in your hearts,
And moved your slow conceptions to rebel?
It must be Korah.   For I see his front
Peering above your dwarf and narrow brows.
He hath inspired this monstrous holiday,
To feed you with the wind of your desires,
And blow you out with vanity.

> [He pushes his way through the Bondmen, fol-
> lowed by some of his companions, the crowd
> of Bondmen being thus split into two parts.
> As he advances, he perceives PELEG, the
> altar, and the sacrificial goat.

                              So! so!
There's more behind this seeming.   I was nigh
To striking at the irritating buzz
Of yonder sacerdotal drone, and letting
The nuisance' self to slip away unhurt.
Workers should sting this idle mouth to death,
That feeds on others' honey, and keeps warm
In comfortable cells the rest contrive.
How dar'st thou, busybody priest, draw off
These toilers from their serviceable task,
To figure in thy feeble pantomime?

FREEMEN.

Now stand aside, ye slaves, nor press around,
But give your betters room to speak and hear.

PELEG.

This is the altar of the Lord, and this
The acceptable sacrifice that turns
His edge of wrath aside.   We sport not here,
But seek to stay His vengeance from your heads,
Ye with yon godless edifice provoke.

ARAN.

Keep your celestial fooling for the hours
When we can spare a chorus for the part.

PELEG (*setting fire to the altar of fagots
from below*).

The Lord decide between us ! for behold
The smoke arises from the ground, and curls
Round and about the ram without a stain.

L

ARAN.

Sonorous charlatan !   Thus do I break

Your paltry toys !

> [He rushes at PELEG, thrusts him aside, and liberates the
> ram.

Now, drive these stray herds home,

Nor spare the whipcord !

> [The Freemen attack the Bondmen, who snatch up the
> kindling brands from the altar to defend themselves.
> PELEG and SIDON retire into different parts of the
> wood.   The Bondmen are soon disarmed and beaten
> and fly towards the Tower, followed by ARAN and
> the Freemen, who flog them as they fly.   SIDON
> alone is left upon the ground, where he contem-
> plates the mangled remains of the ram, which has
> been trampled to death in the fray.

SCENE III

The same hour as in the preceding Scene.   AFRAEL, poised
a league above the Earth.

AFRAEL.

How slowly morning breaks !   It is as though

The air were all on fire, and that the wrack

Were smoke of its wide kindling.   Never yet

Have I beheld such havoc in the sky.
The axis of the round infinite world
Trembles and tilts untrustily; and shakes
The Universe with rude unrhythmic spasms.
Order has been unthronëd in the spheres,
Calm ravished of its crown, and the mute sceptre
Struck from the hand of regal Harmony.
I but surmise where blackly spins the Earth,
For constellation none, nor wandering star,
Spangles the murky cloak that wraps me round.
Yet will unerring instinct thither guide
My unillumined flight; for Love, unhelped,
Straight through the heart of darkness strikes a
        track,
And makes its bourne with certainty.   Now growl,
Ye disproportioned thunders! and ye clouds,
Pile up your shaggy mountains till they bulge
Into the jealous sky's serenest realm,
And make the ether yours!   Let all the air
Confounded be with motions contrary,
Planets roll backward, and the Heavens distend
With loud infernal laughter!   What is it to me,
Who only want one little point of space,
One nook of shelter which the storm must miss,

If only that *she* hides there?   Leave me that,—
And let Creation crumble!

> [He alights upon the Earth, close to the tents of ARAN.
> At the same moment NOEMA comes forth to view
> the morning. ;

SCENE IV

NOEMA.

Now wherefore hast thou come?   Oh! what a dawn!
The air is in the clutches of the wind,
And violently 'gainst its violence
Struggles and shrieks.   Dust, leaves, and waifs of
     nature,
Are whirled and tossed together overhead.
Why hast thou come?   I told thee not to come.
Thou dost not love me, or thou hadst not come!
Thou lovest thyself only.

AFRAEL.

I have a mighty message from the skies.

NOEMA.

About the Tower?

AFRAEL.

No! About thee and me.

Time and Eternity are in thy hands,

To deal with as thou wilt. Thou canst on me

Bestow the flesh-fed flame of mortal life,

And keep it by thee till it be consumed

Unto the final flicker; or thou mayst

Condemn this selfish unsubstantial light

To glow in void unprofitably, through

The weary watches of Eternity.

Quick! speak! then act! and with one magic touch

Transform me into human!

NOEMA.

How? Change to flesh a Spirit! With my arts

Inject a carnal current in thy veins,

Now lightly stirred by rippling purity!

Dull thy bright shape, put thine effulgence out,

And with base body hobble thee to Earth!

O what a foul, vile sorceress should I be,

Sooth could I work such hellish miracle,

If I conceived to do it!

AFRAEL.

But thou must.
The skies consent, and I implore thee to it.

NOEMA.

Never !   Though sky take part against the sky,
And thou against thyself, I will not do it.
I might as well go league with those that build
The irreverent ranges of the rising Tower,
As against Heaven attempt such blasphemy !
But who hath promised thee that I can wield
A power so diabolical ?

AFRAEL.

Voices,
Unseen, untouched, that were but voice alone,
Yet with authoritative cadence spoke.
Come now, essay !   Exert thy mortal love !
For herein, said the Voices, lies thy spell,
And prove it on me !

NOEMA.

'Tis impossible !
For I have no such craft, and if I had,
I would not so abuse it.

AFRAEL.

Then 'tis plain,
Thou dost not love me.

NOEMA.

But I do !

AFRAEL.

Thou dost !
Then bring that vague avowal to a point,
And do with it as thou must do with me,
Making it definite !   Dost think that I,
If I should see thee sinking, would not save ?
And wilt thou unto me, for ever tossed
On the vague sea of space and shoreless time,
Refuse the restful haven of thy heart ?
Tell me thou lov'st me not, and I will go,
A wandering sigh amid the homeless stars.
But if thou love me, love me as Love loves,
And open all thy being !

NOEMA.

Afrael !
How I do love thee, neither human voice

Nor song of Spirit ever could recount.
But Love is not the monarch of the Earth,
Or with one word from his sufficing mouth
Were sorrow swift abolished.   He is but
A poor and scorned conspirator that seeks
To topple down the mighty from their stools.

AFRAEL.

But we would be his co-conspirators,
To——

NOEMA.

——More than share his doom and penalties.
He is immortal, so they cannot kill him,
Maltreat him as they will, and he survives
Their racks and mocks, ever to plot afresh.
But not so they who would assume his cause.
They can be slain outright, or left to live
With mortifying hearts, or,—direst end !—
Buy from convention a deserter's peace,
And creeping to the alien camp become
The loudest of the persecuting train.

AFRAEL.

Then let them slay us !   I am well content
To perish in thy arms, so once I live there !

NOEMA.

See ! I but speak in vain.   Thou art a Spirit
As I so oft have told thee, and the things
Of clay and flesh thou apprehendest not.
I am a slave : I am not free as thou.
I have a husband, a contracted lord,
Who draws my body and service after him,
As, in the patient camel's desert march,
The fore-foot draws the hinder.

AFRAEL.

Dost thou love him ?

NOEMA.

Nay, do not ask !   Can we love what is ill ?
Have I not owned I love thee ?   Let it rest.
For I am his, not thine, and so must keep.
Hadst thou been only Spirit !   Now,—go, go !
Nor let me ever gaze upon thee more,

Till with death's eyes I can serenely look,
And bid thee safe farewell!

AFRAEL.

Not verily!
What! Wilt thou be to me like hard sea-face,
The poor white waves keep climbing fondly up,
Only to fall again?

NOEMA.

I am not hard.
I am too soft; else might you here remain.
But by my softness I beseech you, go!

AFRAEL.

Close once those wild white arms about my form
Then will I go!

NOEMA.

I dare not, Afrael!
Lest chance that fearsome spell begin to work,
The Voices told thee of. Thou fold, instead,
Round me thy heavenly wings, but not for long!
And, when they loosen, then quick take the air,
Ere I have time to wish them back again!

[He folds his wings closely round her.

NOEMA.

Oh ! what bliss !

AFRAEL.

And wilt thou e'er forget me ?

NOEMA.

Never ! till darker wings than thine enfold
This weak outworn automaton of clay,
And I am curtained by oblivion.
Till then, toward thy memory will I gaze,
As in the winter of the world men look
Through bare black branches up to shining stars !
Now, now undo thy wings ! Look ! all the air
Grows murk and dense ! Thou wilt not see thy way.
Go ! I abjure thee !—go !

AFRAEL.

Farewell ! Farewell !
But shouldst thou ever call me in thy need,
Thy voice will reach me, and my broken wings
Will flutter towards thee !

[He ascends, and is instantly lost in the murky air.

SCENE V

*The tents of ARAN.   A terrific tempest and thunderstorm.
Enter ARAN in hot haste.*

ARAN (*alone*).

The Heavens have heard our challenge, and take up
The note of our defiance.   Hark ! on high,
The thunderous roll of hollow-bowelled clouds
Sounds the attack.   Where art thou, Noema ?
The welkin moves in surly masses on
Before the march of the sky's armëd hosts,
Hidden as yet behind the dust of war.
Shortly we shall behold the embattled lines,
And Heaven and Earth be locked in wrestling grip,
And see who throws the other.   Noema !
Where doth she skulk ?   How hisses the swift hail !
As yet they shoot their javelins from afar,
Wasting their shafts in showy bravery.
Celestial madmen ! husband up your points,
Till to close quarters ye have come, for then
Ye'll need them all !   Why ! what weak bolts are
     these,

That scarce would scare the turtle to her nest?

Ha! that was better!   They wax nearer now!

Welcome, ye overt enemies that thus

Announce your coming.   We will meet you.   Lo!

That ragged flash rent the creased rack in twain,

And yet I did not see them!   How was that?

I should have caught the glimmer of their files

Through that tremendous opening.   What a peal!

It was a bellow fit to shake the spheres;

And sooth the Earth did quake.   But not with dread,—

Think not, with dread!—ye noisy emissaries!

Come on, and we will prove you, foot to foot,

And if we cannot shout as loud as you,

We'll strike the harder.   Where is Noema?

Never at hand at need!   I want my spear;

The same that, wedded to my passion, hath

In many a foray split the raging boar,

And to the jungle sent the hyæna scotched.

Now shall it dip its beak in loftier gore.

[He stumbles over NOEMA.

Ha! there thou art!   What! again sunk in swoon,

When hubbub is enough o'erhead to wake

The leaden-dreaming dead.   Well, sleep thou there

Till it blows over.   'Tis a feeble heart,

Just fit to bear the note of victory,
But not the bray of battle.   Louder still !
That crash must be the prelude.   Ha ! my spear !
And I shall be in time !   They'll hold till then.
Bristles the Tower, compact, from head to foot.
Upon each circling balcony I left
A regiment all armed, and on the top
The bravest of my friends with eager edge
Await the onset.   At the base are drawn
Dense cohorts in reserve, whom I will pour,
Upward by stair and corridor, to take
The place of those hurled headlong, so that never
A gap shall spoil our ranks, but they shall push
Wedgewise to Heaven !

                                   [Enter IRAD.

IRAD.

            O father ! what a storm !

ARAN.

Ay, boy ! it is a very noble storm.
Wilt face it with me ?

IRAD.

            Yes, if mother wills.

ARAN.

Heed not thy mother now! This is no time
To borrow leave from women. Wilt come, my lad?
I'm going to the Tower, and thou shalt, too.

IRAD.

But mother would be vexed.

ARAN.

Go to thy mother!
And whine and gab with women all thy life.
Thou art a girl disguised!

IRAD.

Then I will go, father!

ARAN.

Quick, then! for time is pricking at our heels.
Give me thy hand! Be nimble with thy limbs;
And show in every aspect of thy gait,
That Aran is thy father!

[Exeunt.

SCENE VI

The Tower.   Every compartment and balcony crowded with
    armed men.   EBER, unarmed, on a coign of vantage,
    half-way up, surveying the storm.   Round the base,
    crowds likewise of armed men ; and amongst these, but
    without armour, PELEG, KORAH, and SIDON.

PELEG.

See what it is to rise against the Lord,
And dare His wrath omnipotent !   He frowns,
And straight the whirlwinds spread their wings and
        wreak
Their ravage on ye !   Lo ! He stamps His foot,
And mighty-mouthëd thunders, roused from sleep,
Come growling from their lair !   Lay down your arms,
Ere they be stricken from your paltry hands,
Or their points turned against ye !   On your knees,
And, with your foreheads burrowed in the dust,
Clamour for pardon !

SOME.

            Ay, 'twere best !   For look !

The Heavens with rage wax purple.   Surely, then,
The ground did rock ?

OTHERS.

                    Ay, that it did !   But wait !
'Tis but a storm at worst.   Prayer will not lay it.
Nay, let us, friends, be valiant to the last,
And bide the upshot.

SIDON.

                    'Tis a tempest only.
For Nature hath grown fractious, and contends
Against herself.   Eber will tell us why,
When this her wanton mood hath rolled away.'
Look where he's perched, and with impassive eye
Scans her vagaries, just as though he were
Carved and incorporate with the edifice !
'Tis a brave sight ; and not with looks alone,
But with your deeds commend him.   Wait and see
What this explosive termagant, this Nature,
Means by her tears, her gestures, and her shrieks.
These are the empty imprecations hurled
By the infuriate Void.   'Twill pass away,

                    M

As violence doth ever.   As for prayer,
Think you it would be heard in such a din?
Look on and learn, or else to bed and sleep
Until it slumbers.   Ye can do no more.
Either were something.

> [The fierceness of the tempest increases; the thunder
> rolls louder; and the earth is shaken violently.

PELEG.

On your knees, I say!
And imitate the instinctive fowls that crouch,
When blows the hurricane.

SOME.

What say ye?

OTHERS.

No!

Let us hold on at least till Aran comes.
Where is he, now?

KORAH.

Why, gone, I warrant ye,
To strike a private bargain for himself
With foes he hath provoked and cannot match.

SOME.

Think ye that's so?

OTHERS.

Tush! Korah's jealous tongue
Invents a coward.   Aran is as brave
As loftiest cedar that on loftiest top
Of Ararat ne'er budges, though the storm
Tears up the soil it stands on.

KORAH.

But if not,
And Aran seeks no safety for himself,
See to your own!   Cry out to Eber there
To crave a parley with the skies.   This war,
With its abhorrent front and threatening face,
Against your peaceful destiny offends.
Throw down your arms, and call upon the Heavens
To lay down theirs.   Patch up a treaty quick,
And swear the heralds of the upper world
Not to molest ye more, but leave the Earth
To its own shifts and purposes, as ye
Will henceforth leave the spheres.   Thus will ye keep
An open Future for yourselves, wherein

Man may pursue uninterruptedly
His pathway to Perfection.

SOME.

Aran comes!
Look where he cleaves the mist!

OTHERS.

And with him brings
The little Irad, who steps bravely out
And lags behind his father's stalwart stride,
No further than one's shadow.

ALL.

Hail to stout Aran, Builder of the Tower!
Long live man's truest leader!

ARAN.

Was it you,
Or the Heaven's braggart thunders that I heard?
These vultures of the welkin seem to think
To scare us with their shrieking! Ye do well
To pay them noise for noise. Now clash your shields,
So that they cannot fail to know ye are here,
And thrill to meet the vanguard of their strokes,

With such impatience as the bridegroom feels

For the first shock of rapture !

> [Those at the foot of the Tower clash their shields, and
> the action is imitated by the armed hosts on each
> storey in succession, to the very top.   Almost
> simultaneously there is a fresh peal of thunder,
> louder and longer than any of the preceding ones.

Music for music !   But I like yours best !

The Heavens have heard your cymbals clang, and roll

Their drums to answer ye !   Now, quick, come forth,

Ye slow supernal athletes, and make good

The tumult of your challenge !   We are here,

And Earth's smooth dust is ready to receive

The thud of your celestial overthrow !

> [As he speaks, lightning strikes the summit of the Tower,
> and, amidst the roar of thunder, the topmost storeys
> with their armed defenders are hurled headlong
> through the air, crushing, as they reach the ground,
> many of those collected at the base ; amongst these,
> PELEG and SIDON.   Some of the survivors fly from
> the ground.   Others crowd fearfully round ARAN.

ARAN.

Why do ye shake, ye aspen-wooded hearts,

At the first breath of battle ?   Let them fly,

Those mock-heroic supernumeraries !

What want we with their fluttering pulses here ?

They shall be bondmen when the battle's done,
When ye shall rule as Gods! Hold firm, up there,
On ledge, and balcony, and jutting coign!
Ye have the post of honour now, nor yield
One inch of what ye hold! Dream not to save
Your lives by coming lower! By this spear,
If any thinks to fly from death at top,
He'll find it at the bottom! Do ye deem,
I who have brought this unarmed baby here
To sniff the risky breath of victory,
Will let *men* shirk the tussle?

> [He perceives the dead body of PELEG.

                             Ha! what is this?
Peleg as dead as sacrificial kid!
Pretentious Priest, how empty art thou now!
But what a pack of blundering combatants
Not to know friend from foe! The clumsy Heavens!

> [Kicking the body aside.

He is their dead, and they must bury him,
When we've done fighting. What! And Sidon, too!
A stale conclusion to thy arguments!
Priest, and Philosopher, by one blind bolt

Hit and confounded !   There is humour then

In these celestial strokes.

> [A fresh peal is heard, and several more storeys, injured
> by the previous shock, are toppled down ; EBER
> among those who fall.

What ! struck again !

See ! here comes Eber, like a falling star !

He'll soon be out !

Now, death ! and ruin ! what is this base work ?

Come forth, ye skulking Spirits, ye curs of Heaven !

Out from your opaque ambush, and descend

In visible battalions on our points !

This is but cowards' work !

KORAH.

Leave him, friends !

Hear how he raves !   It was a madman's hand

Piled up the Tower, a madman who defends.

Away, and keep yourselves for better days !

What's Heaven to you, who still have got the Earth ?

'Ware lest ye lose them both !

ARAN.

How, insolent !

Thou wouldst incite my legions to desert,

And march towards the Future !   March there thou !

> [He pierces KORAH with his spear, who falls.

But travel unaccompanied! Thou art
Perfected now, for thou hast surely touched
The goal of all things! . . . Now, ye craven imps,
Angel or devils, gods or mercenaries
Of some one God more potent than yourselves,
Slaves of the sky, purveyors of the thunder,
Ye noisy rabble of the clouds! appear
Afront our serried infantry, that we
May drive you homeward, following at your heels!
Dare none of you be patent? Why, I thought
'Twas only women hid behind their veils!

> [A thunder-crash is heard more violent than any gone
> before. The ground rocks and splits. IRAD, who
> has till now remained scared but silent by his father's
> side, utters a cry. AFRAEL swoops through the air
> towards him.

Ha! Here is one of them at last! Now, taste
The savour of my spear, which those shall chew
Who follow after thee!

> [He strikes at AFRAEL with his spear, which catches a
> flash of lightning on its point, and ARAN falls, a
> blackened carcass. AFRAEL bears IRAD into the
> air. Seeing ARAN fall, those still at the base of
> the Tower fly in all directions, whilst those left
> above hurry down, and do the same. The storm
> begins to abate and die away.

SCENE VII

The tents of ARAN.

NOEMA (*waking from her swoon*).

What was that sound?   Methought I heard a crash
As though the Earth were splitting.   And how dark
And weird it is, even here!   I must have swooned,
Again have swooned.   Ho!   Aran!   Art thou there?
He answers not.   To the accursëd Tower,
As daily, hath he gone.   Irad!   Irad!
Where art thou, Irad?   If there brews a storm,
He waits for it to burst, with eager eyes
Facing the tempest.

[She goes to the front of the chief tent.

But look! the Tower has vanished!   Irad!   Aran!
Irad! where art thou, Irad?   Where is my boy?
Oh! he hath gone, whilst I was blind in swoon,
And in the rage that whelms the wicked found
An innocent's destruction!

[She runs back into the tents, and hurries to and fro.

Irad!   Irad!

Art thou there, Irad?   Shout but once to me,

And I shall know thou livest.   What!   No voice!
No sound!   Not here! not here!   Oh! he is dead,
And I—— It is his voice!

[IRAD rushes in.

IRAD.

Mother! mother!

[He rushes into the arms of NOEMA, who folds him to
her heart; and for a moment both are silent.

NOEMA.

Where hast thou been?

IRAD.

He bade me, and I went
With father to the Tower.

NOEMA.

And where is he?

IRAD.

Father is dead.

NOEMA.

Dead!

IRAD.

Yes, and thousands more,
Buried beneath the Tower.

NOEMA.

Didst see it fall?

IRAD.

Yes! and with such a crash—once—twice!—and men
Fell through the air in flocks. And how it
    thundered!
Mother, you never heard how loud it thundered!
And all the time the zigzag lightnings flashed,
And the ground heaved and swayed, and every one
Was sore afraid, save father; and he died,
Daring the Heavens to fight him.

NOEMA.

Died as he lived,
Defiant and unbroken!

IRAD.

When the Tower
Had fallen, and those who fell with it and those

On whom it fell, were or dashed down or crushed,—
Eber, and Peleg, Sidon, thousands more,—
Then all began to scatter, save a few
Who stood by father; and I stood by him.
But Korah sought to make these others fly,
Deserting father's side, and father slew him.

NOEMA.

With his own hand?

IRAD.

                    Yes, mother! with his spear.
And then it was that the Earth split and shook,
And I who had been terrified from first,
But did my best to stifle every cry,
Not to vex father, gave a girlish scream,
And some one, not a mortal, clove the air,
And father thrust at him, but thrust in vain,
And fell as though by lightning hit, and scorched,
And charred all in a moment! while, as swift,
He who had swooped upbore me through the air,
As a gerfalcon bears a suckling lamb,
But with such tender clutches, that I seemed
Only to be, mother, rocked upon your breast.

And when we had gone up, a little way,
Soft he sailed down again, and set me here,
Here at my dear, dear home.　Mother! mother!

[Afrael appears.

SCENE VIII

NOEMA.

It was no flash of thine, smote Aran dead?

AFRAEL.

I have no power of death ; and if I had,
On him I had not used it.

NOEMA.

Thank Heaven for that !　But it was he, was struck
And shrivelled at the instant of thy swoop
To snatch up Irad.

AFRAEL.

Then I saw him fall,
Blistered and burnt and blackened all at once.
He caught a shred of lightning on his spear,

Consumed by what he captured.   That was Aran !
Well, he died bravely.

NOEMA.

Go, Afrael, go ! for I am very sad.
Return, when Time hath quieted my pain,
And the distraction of this hour shall be,
Like yon late tempest, over.   Not till then !
Come when the moon is next, as now, at full ;
And choose the same sweet moment as when first
I heard your voice and hailed it.

                              [He ascends into the sky.

END OF ACT IV

ACT V

SCENE I

The air.   Midsummer.   Late evening twilight, through
which the moon rises, at full.

AFRAEL (*alone*).

THE night, the hour have come! O long, long
    Moon,
How I have waited for thee to refill
Thy pale dim outline with clear rounded light!
Now thou art full and fervent.   And shall not
This pale dim Me, this shadowy nothingness,
This tenuous adumbration of delight,
Be with substantial aspect and real glow
Filled in, like thee?   Now farewell, heavenly space!
Farewell, thou vault sublime!   Farewell, ye stars,
That hold the keys of fixëd harmony.
Forget me not!   I never will forget ye!

Over that new and lesser home which waits
My transformation, watch with constant ray,
Nor me desert, deserter though I be,
And for her gentle sake propitious shine,
For whom I quit ye !

SCENE II

Same hour.   The tents of NOEMA.

NOEMA (*alone*).

It seems like yesternight that I sate here,
And saw him first.   The spot, the hour, and see !
The self-same face of Heaven !   How beautiful !
Yet in all else how utterly unlike
That then from now !   Oh ! I am terrified !
Why placed I so ephemeral a bar
Betwixt me and his coming?   It is sure
That he will come !   He never failed me yet.
What, if he did !   Then I should call for him,
And leave the sky no quiet till he came.

[Afrael appears.

SCENE III

In the moonlight.

NOEMA.

Afrael !

AFRAEL.

Yes, I am here, true as yon rounded moon,
To countenance my coming.

NOEMA.

Oh, 'tis soon.

Keep silent for a while !

AFRAEL.

Too late, too late
Thou tellest me to be silent.   I have taken
Of the Eternal Heavens eternal leave,
And bidden the stars farewell.

NOEMA.

Oh ! no ! no ! no !
Look up !   Look up !   Remember thy abode,

N

And contemplate those interspersëd orbs,
The golden gleams on yon lake lazulite,
The glittering gems on the all-circling crown
Of Majesty Eternal !   Lift thy gaze
Back unto those, not lower it down on me,
Where thou wilt but a crude amalgam find
Of dust and yearning.   If a falling star
Never touched aught but darkness, how wilt thou
Reach light and life by such an ebon plunge ?

AFRAEL.

Didst ever see a star that tried to turn ?
I will not back !   I have left Void for Heaven !
And in these wings, I call thee to annul,
For the last time I fold thee !

> [As his wings encircle her, she folds her arms around
> him, and they kiss.

NOEMA.

Afrael !

AFRAEL.

See, they are fading now, and in their place
Live definite members come.   I feel the rush
As of a thousand torrents through my being,

But torrents at volcanic sources warmed.

And now I burn and shiver all at once.

Canst thou not feel me now, as ne'er before?

For I, as ne'er before, do now feel thee.

NOEMA.

Yes! Thou art waxing human to my touch,

And thee intensely do I see, hear, know,

As though thou wert myself!

AFRAEL.

And so I am!

SCENE IV

A week later. Sundown. The tents of AFRAEL and NOEMA.

NOEMA.

Sit by me here, and tell me is it true

They speak with divers tongues, and understand

One not the other?

AFRAEL.

'Tis conceivable.

Nought is so unintelligent as fear,
For, while it speaks with obscure stammering lips,
It comprehends not what is plainly said.
You cannot parley with it.   Thus will it fare
Ever with their temerity who think
To storm and raze the Unknown. Preposterous Towers,
Absolute wreck, and tongues' confusion,—
Such, through all change of circumstance and time,
Will be their brief and doleful history !

NOEMA.

Have you no sure conception how the Tower
Was overthrown ?   Whether a frolic troop
Of Seraphim invisible rode by,
And with the point of their light-poisèd spears
Tilted, and down it went ?   Or lightnings real,
With thunder in reserve, successive launched
By Heaven's almighty Captain, smote its front,
And routed its pretenders ?

AFRAEL.

                    Who shall say ?
I saw no armoured Seraphim, nor heard
Thunders unparalleled or lightnings strange,

But only complete sickness of the air,

Clouds vomiting fire, and with deep rumblings vexed,

To which the Earth responded; and the Tower

Collapsed in their commotion.   It may be

That one of Nature's mindless accidents

The ruin wrought; or that the Unseen Power

Made that loud music with man's folly chime,

And with a fixed coincidence rebuked

His weak extravagance.   We cannot know.

Even in that star whose denizen I was

Ere Earth's more blest inhabitant I turned,

God's face was all as dim as seems it here.

How were it otherwise?   Let finite feet

With straining breath and clamorous tongue pursue,

With faster feet Infinity recedes,

And we drop ever more behind the view,

Which ere we started it, was very close;

Ay, if we do not frighten it away,

By prying if 'tis there, still keeps a seat

In every human breast.   What though the Earth

May not ascend to Heaven, by Tower or aught

Of man's devising, Heaven descends to Earth

For those who will receive it.   We have it here,

Here in each other's arms, where Spirit and flesh

Have recognised their kinship.   Love is nought
But shadow or mere carcass, save it blend
The breath of both :—a name, a nothingness,
Or wholly self and bestial.

NOEMA.

There it is !
Spirit is not extinguished by the flesh,
'Nor flesh repelled by Spirit.   One is flame,
The other fuel ; both are requisite
For Love's unfading fire.   That is a truth,
A Being well might abdicate the skies,
To learn, and teach.

AFRAEL.

And thou hast taught it me.
My Noema, good-night !   Sound be thy sleep !

NOEMA.

And sweet, thine, Afrael !   My love, good-night !

THE END

Printed by R & R. CLARK, *Edinburgh*

Now Publishing in Monthly Volumes.

Volume I. December 1890.

A COLLECTED EDITION

OF

THE POETICAL WORKS OF

MR. ALFRED AUSTIN

In 6 volumes, crown 8vo, price 5s. each.

THE TOWER OF BABEL.   [*Ready.*

SAVONAROLA.

SATIRES, ETC.

PRINCE LUCIFER.

THE HUMAN TRAGEDY.

LYRICAL POEMS.

MACMILLAN AND CO., LONDON.